Killing Our Grandchildren

Peter Brickwood

Published by peter brickwood, 2022.

This is a work of fiction. Similarities to real people, places, or events are entirely coincidental.

KILLING OUR GRANDCHILDREN

First edition. May 24, 2022.

Written by Peter Brickwood.

FridaysForFuture

Chapter One

"Fracking is killing our grandchildren. Burning oil is killing..."

Gus touched the long gun under his buttoned coat and felt the reassuring pressure of the four revolvers. Impatiently he waited for the invitation checker to give him his credential. He watched the room packed with stockholders. Finally, the clerk handed him his pass. He retrieved all his papers, not wanting to leave anything that could later be examined for prints, DNA or even clues about the source of the paper or ink of the invitation he had fabricated.

He moved into the meeting room and stepped quickly along the back wall, undoing his long raincoat as he went. The young woman at the microphone continued to harangue the corporation's officers. 'Gorgeous red hair,' thought Gus. *Stay focused*. He began moving down the side of the room.

"...so what actions are you taking?" the speaker finished her question and stood glaring at the row of old white men. Gus stepped into the space between the front row and the head table and began to spray with his long gun. Emptying it, he dropped the gun on its carrying strap and turned up the center aisle toward the back of the room. Pulling a revolver from under each shoulder, he began targeting the most excitable members of the audience.

On his right, a timid fellow scrambling out of a row got a slug in his back. A woman on his left with an obnoxiously pink dress screamed as a shot hit her. Halfway to the back of the room, Gus slammed the revolvers into holsters without noticing a clatter as he came to a dead stop in front of the microphone. 'Truly beautiful,' he thought. Under the mane of red hair was a freckled face with no hint of apprehension and a curve of incredulous laughter forming on her lips.

Coming to his senses, Gus swung past her, pulled the second pair of pistols and shot randomly into the crowd before pushing out of the door. Holstering the revolvers, he strode across the lobby and through a street door, adding the wail of fire alarms to the general confusion.

Gus tugged a hat from his pocket and began stuffing his unruly hair into it as he walked briskly along the sidewalk. He muttered, "Stay in step with everyone else and don't draw attention," like a mantra until halfway down the second block, where he was able to turn into a rather narrow alley between two buildings. Fortunately, nobody was putting out garbage or having a smoke so he marched straight toward the other end.

He pulled an industrial strength black garbage bag from another pocket, and then slapped the quick release on his holster gear. Shrugging out of the raincoat and holsters, he stuffed everything into the bag. He took a lightweight shell out of the suit jacket's side pocket and held it in his teeth while he ripped off his tie and struggled out of the suit jacket. Jamming them into the bag, he hastily closed it by knotting the top. With the shell in one hand, the bag in the other, Gus left the alley.

As he turned onto the main street, he glimpsed a streetcar coming towards him. A construction dumpster was where he expected it and he threw his bag of guns and clothes into it without anyone challenging him. He hoped the whole load would soon be on its way to a landfill where his prints and DNA would be buried forever.

Struggling to appear unhurried, Gus continued along the street towards the streetcar stop. He shook out the shell and pulled it over his head. Stepping up onto the streetcar, he dropped in the correct change, then moved down the aisle to slide into a seat behind the back door. Gus glanced through the car's back windows in what he hoped was a casual manner. Seeing nothing that looked like pursuit, he thought, 'So far so good.'

After traveling several blocks, the car shunted and banged a couple of times then the driver called out, "There's an accident in the next intersection so we won't be moving for an hour or more."

Passengers got down from the streetcar and walked toward the intersection. Gus joined the people crossing the street then looked back. Still no sign of pursuit as he set off at a brisk pace. 'Not quite how I planned it.' But his tactical voice reassured him, *No other option and minimal impact on the schedule.*

When he arrived at a large bicycle rental depot, Gus used a key to open a locker and took out a daypack. Slinging the bag over his shoulder, he crossed into a washroom. Quickly he pulled off his dress shoes, pants and shirt then got into a tee shirt and shorts. As he was about to put on a pair of trainers his voice reminded him: *Replace your dress socks with sports socks.*

Outside, he took out a pass card for the bike rental system, swiped it over a lock and lifted the released machine clear. With his pack on his shoulders, he turned the bike and pushed it towards the exit. Gus noticed a young woman rattling a bike that was stuck in its rack. *Stay on task.* His eyes took in long brown legs, white shorts, a close-fitting tee and smooth blond hair pulled back into a ponytail. 'What harm can it do to offer help?' *You should not be noticeable; do not leave someone who can identify you.*

"Having a problem?" Gus asked.

"I do not understand. I put in the money but it does not come out." Waving her hands in frustration, she turned toward him.

"Sometimes the locks stick. Let's get a different one, which would you like?"

"I have no more money." Smiling, she found the correct words. "Umm. I have no more coins; no change."

"That's all right, I have a bulk pass." *Which will register two uses at this rack, which will set them to searching for a witness.*

"Oh, that is very kind," she said, as he released a bike for her with his card. "How can I repay you?"

"Well, you can tell me where that lovely accent comes from." *Oh, you silver-tongued devil, now she'll remember you for sure.*

"Ah, I am Dutch. Which way do you go?" she asked with another dazzling smile.

Dumbstruck, he gestured to the right. Apparently accustomed to such responses she asked, "That is the way to the picnic, umm, barn?"

He could only nod as she stepped up onto her pedal and pushed off. Belatedly, he jumped onto his bike and joined her.

"Uh, the shelter. Umm we call it a picnic shelter. You're meeting your boyfriend?"

With a light laugh she told him, "No. No. Just friends, it is a celebration. My friend is in Holland." Laughing outright when his face fell, she went on, "Truly I don't have a boyfriend. That was mmm, bad? Cruel? Mean?"

"Perhaps a little unkind," he said, as a happier smile came onto his face.

They whizzed along the path animatedly talking about the engineering feats of the Dutch, clearing plastic from inland waters and land reclamation. All too soon, he braked to a stop and pointed out a path. "That's the way to the picnic area."

"Would you like to join us?" she asked with another dazzling smile.

"I'd love to..." the tactical voice, in the back of his head, started up again, *Uh ah. No way. You...* "but I have work that must be finished tonight."

"Oh, what a pity, I go back to the Netherlands tomorrow. It has been nice meeting you." She began to turn her bike towards the side path.

"Uhmm. Perhaps I could write to you?"

"Oh yes, please give me your phone."

"Well no. I mean I'll be off grid for quite a while. Do you have a mailing address?"

"Mailing?"

"Yes, umm post, like a letter, in an envelope with a stamp." He pulled out a piece of paper and wrote his P.O. Box address on it then mimed licking a stamp and mailing an envelope.

"Oh yes." Chuckling she took his address and pulled a photo booth picture out of her bag and wrote her address on the back. She held it up to ask, "You like my picture?"

"Very much."

"Good. This way you will be able to remember which of your many conquests I am."

"I don't... I mean," Gus stammered and blushed, hearing her laugh as she sailed away down the path.

"Send good stamps, my little brother loves stamps," she called over her shoulder before disappearing around a curve.

Gazing after her, he began to clamber onto his bicycle. *OH. Are we going to get back on task now?* Gus felt a little hollow riding on towards the end of the path but picked up his pace. Hopping off, he racked the bike then walked away with a jaunty step. Two blocks up, he came to a cab rank. Climbing into the first taxi, he told the driver to take him to a mall, which was near the western edge of the city.

"OK man, I can do that," said the driver as he started off. "This time of day the side streets are better. That OK with you?"

The driver looked expectantly into the rear-view mirror.

"Uh? Oh yeah, sure," Gus replied and went back to daydreaming about a European romance.

The Netherlands, world leader in flood control and hydroponic farming. 'It would be nice to have a guided tour with a beautiful girl.' *Only guided tour you're going to get is of the local jail if you don't pay attention.* Startled, he realized the taxi was pulling into a parking space. He dug a couple of twenties out and passed them to the driver.

"Keep the change."

"Hey, thanks man, have a..."

Gus was already hustling in through the swing doors. That tip was too generous. He'll remember you. 'Yeah, yeah.' Gus went straight through the mall to a regional bus terminal. He got a ticket from the automatic kiosk, just in time to catch the on-the-hour bus into a nearby suburb.

As the adrenalin high wore off, Gus dozed in his seat. The bus's arrival jolted him awake; climbing down off the bus he shoved his hands in his pockets and began to walk away. *Change your profile, get the shell off and put the ball cap on backwards.* His own hyper security annoyed him but he pulled off the shell then loitered by the tinted windows of the terminal. Seeing nothing to concern him, he set off again. The sun was bright, so he kept his cap peak forward to shade his eyes as he walked along his pre-planned route, up and around a couple of side streets, doubling back once. Still nothing to concern him. 'Although I've only seen this in movies, so how would I know what should make me suspicious?' he mused.

Entering the small private hotel, he spied the pretty receptionist. *No flirting.* His tactical voice was emphatic.

"Hello, how was your day?"

"OK," she replied. "The best part is I'm off soon."

"Could I have my key please?" Taking it he turned away saying, "Have a nice evening."

"You too," she replied with professional brightness.

Gus closed the door to his room and gazed longingly at the bed. 'A nap would be good.' *Trim your hair to a quarter inch, in the tub. Take a shower. Make sure all the hair clippings are gone. Pack up everything you used today into a garbage bag and anything else you don't need. Make sure your clothes are laid out, your daypack is ready, and the alarm is set for tomorrow.* The voice droned on relentlessly.

Before getting started, he used the remote to turn on the TV. The small, privately-owned hotel was out of the way but could be easily identified if he used any of his own electronics. Groaning, he set to work. Three quarters of an hour later, he came out of the bathroom to see the end of a news promo. Grabbing the remote, he cranked the sound up in hopes of catching the next bulletin.

By the time the news began, he had sanitized the room to the best of his ability. Everything was in garbage bags except the wrapping on the sandwich he would eat for supper and his soda can. He settled down to watch the news. His earlier exploit was not mentioned on the national news as he had hoped. 'The regional news would be better than nothing,' he thought. Disappointed by the end of the local news, he rationalized that there must be a news blackout until an investigation was completed. Gus crawled under the covers and dropped into an exhausted sleep.

'Argh, what is that awful noise?' His mind clawed up through grasping shrouds of sleep as he banged his feet onto the floor. Coming suddenly awake, Gus scrambled from his bed in fright. *Easy, easy, it is just the alarm clock.* Gus calmed as he remembered where he was. *You got away clean. Nobody is breaking in to arrest you.* He clicked on the television again but there was nothing to interest him so he went into the bathroom to have a shower. Dressing, he watched the news hopefully but there was still nothing. 'My action should have been important enough for local television, at least,' he thought.

Gus put his key and a tip on the sideboard then carefully looked around the room to make sure he had not forgotten anything. Satisfied, he hoisted his main pack onto his back and grabbed the garbage bag in one hand and his daypack in the other. Getting down the back stairs and out the parking lot door was awkward but he managed it without too much noise.

The large green bag made walking difficult, and he wondered what he would do with it if the drivers had changed their schedule. Turning a corner, he smiled with relief at the row of garbage trucks idling in the street while their drivers got coffee and donuts. As he went past, Gus threw his garbage bag into the back of a truck.

He joined the line at the bus stop, flexing his hand to get the circulation back. 'Always the same,' he thought, 'at five AM the people are all black, brown, and yellow. Not a suit and tie in sight.' The express bus pulled up. Worried he would fall asleep; he took a seat under the loudspeaker so the annoying synthetic voice would wake him at his stop. As he got off, Gus checked his watch; realizing he was a little late, he jogged toward his destination.

He need not have worried. When he arrived at the assembly area people were milling around, yawning, looking for washrooms, searching for friends and generally engaging in the convivial chaos of setting out on a trip that promised to be a bit of an adventure.

Gus consumed a muffin and two coffees before things got started. A friendly guy with a clipboard told the group to come forward when he called their first name, hand over their registration forms, then stow their baggage in the luggage bay of a touring bus.

When Gus's name was called, he easily slid his main pack into the hold under the bus and climbed aboard. Finding a seat by a window, halfway back, he settled in. Then he saw her coming down the aisle toward him. No mistaking that mane of red hair. She stopped and tossed a pistol into his lap.

"You dropped this."

Chapter Two

Gus looked around quickly. The bus had started up and was rolling toward the ramp leading to the highway. *No chance of getting off without making a huge scene.* He slid the pistol under his leg as he glanced back and forth but nobody seemed to be paying any attention to them.

She seated herself beside him. Smiling sweetly, she said, "You wrecked my question, you know."

He gazed into her clear blue eyes under the wild red hair, again noticing the freckles spreading across the smooth skin of her cheeks.

"It had taken me weeks to develop a question they couldn't wriggle out of. Then you blew up that meeting! Still, it was funny to watch all that lime green goop dripping off their faces."

Gus snapped out of his daze and made a downward motion with his palm. "Could you keep it down please? They use public mischief charges to send people to prison for doing that kind of stuff."

She paused, drawing together her brows. "A person who hid your gun could be charged as an accessory. Even if it was a squirt gun."

"Well, I don't think..."

This time she cut him off. "Don't know many cops or prosecutors do you? They tend to think in terms of Catholic mothers hiding IRA guns in baby prams." Pursing her lips, she looked around.

Gus said, "I'll get rid of it." He bent to fit the gun into his daypack and pulled out a deck of cards. Trying to calm the conversation, he asked her, "Care to play?"

"Whoa, retro. Actual cardboard."

"No cell phones or Wi-Fi where we're going."

Just then, the cheerful chubby fellow with the clipboard stood up at the front and used the coach's loudspeaker system to get the passengers attention. "Thank you all for being here. Plastic Reuse appreciates you volunteering a month of your time. There will be a rest stop a couple of hours up the highway. Just a few quick notes from me for now: We should get to the base camp by tomorrow evening. That is where you will get two or three days of training and then set out for the actual work camp. Tonight, we'll stay at a motel near Lake End. As you know, we pride ourselves on protecting your anonymity, so we recommend using first names only. Any questions?"

Someone near the back called out, "Why use this fancy coach? Seems like an unnecessarily heavy carbon footprint." Some concerned head nodding greeted this statement.

"It's a trade-off between getting everybody together in a reasonable amount of time and creating more CO_2 than we would want to," explained the trip leader. "Plastic Reuse is part of an umbrella group that has a tree planting operation which it finances with government funding for carbon offset credits. We buy the credits for dirty diesel trips like this from them so that ultimately the government funds our bus ride." There were a couple of chuckles, and the explanation seemed to satisfy everyone, so the trip leader added, "I'll be around to talk to you all individually, as we travel."

Gus's seat mate said, "I'm Lee by the way," offering her hand.

"Gus," he answered, taking hers. Neither released the other's hand.

After a few moments Lee said, "It is going to be awkward playing with those cards. Do you like crossword puzzles?"

"Sure," he replied. Gradually their hands parted and Lee found her tablet.

"Do you think the carbon credit program is effective?" asked Gus, not that he cared at that moment, but he felt a need to fill the space between them.

She looked thoughtful as she opened a crossword puzzle app then responded, "I suppose so, within the confines of its intent." As the touring coach roared along, they spent more time in conversation than solving clues.

The slowing of the bus surprised both of them. Looking out of the window, Gus noticed a rather grubby independent gas station then a large children's play area as the coach turned into an oversized parking space in a mini-mall lot. Everyone jostled off the bus in a good-natured race for the washrooms.

"Get me a snack, would you? And meet me at the picnic table by the jungle gym."

"OK. What are..." she started to ask, but he was already striding toward the gas station.

The washroom door he had seen from the bus was locked but with a hard twist of the handle and quick bang with his shoulder, he popped the lock. Gus quickly destroyed the gun; as he was exiting the washroom, he almost bumped into an attendant. With his head down he mumbled, "Sorry man, I really had to go."

Lee had seated herself at a picnic table. As he walked toward her, Gus dropped a paper bag into a three-quarters full garbage barrel and tramped on towards the table. Dropping onto the bench opposite Lee, he smiled, saying, "All gone."

"What, you just tossed it in the garbage?" she asked in a somewhat agitated voice.

"No." Seeing she needed more of an explanation, he continued, "There were rags and bleach in the washroom. I took it apart and scrubbed it down with the rags then dropped it in the sink with hot water and bleach. Let it soak for a minute then pulled it out. I broke it into small pieces which I put into the paper bag you saw me throw into a garbage pail." He jerked his head towards the play area.

"Shouldn't be any usable prints, fibers or DNA. Difficult to demonstrate a chain of connection to us." She pondered for a moment then said, "All right. Thanks."

"You know a lot about the legal stuff."

"Yeah, I'm in pre-law."

"Ah. I see. If you were charged with a felony, you could not be called to the bar. Good of you to take the risk for me."

"I didn't even know you when I took the risk."

"Uh." Slightly deflated, he looked down at the table. "What's this?"

"You asked for a snack and a drink."

"Yeah but a banana and water. In a plastic bottle?"

"It's hemp plastic, I checked."

"Still, I was thinking more like coffee and a donut."

He ate the banana and glugged down water as they walked back to the bus. A petite blond smiled at him as they approached the doors.

"Don't feel obliged to sit with me," Lee said as he led the way to their seats.

Puzzled, he answered, "Well, I'd like to take a nap so you can have the window seat if you like." He half stood in the aisle seat to let her pass. Lee took care not to brush up against him as she moved to the window seat. Nonetheless, he enjoyed the fragrance of her shampoo.

Slumping into his seat, he was asleep within moments. The bus rolled through farmlands into woodlands and on through rugged rocky forest. Some hours later Gus awoke suddenly. Startled, he looked around swiftly until his gaze settled on her.

"Sorry, I tried to wake you gently."

"Ah. Yeah. I always wake up like that."

"You know you snore."

"Umm. Does that mean you won't share a room with me?"

"I'll share a room with you," Lee said, seeming to startle herself. She regarded him with her clear blue eyes and added, "But you do know you could share with almost any of these girls."

He was spared responding to her comment because the bus bumped through potholes as it pulled into another rest stop. The trip leader announced, "Biological break. There is a great outlook point where you can see Lake End, but we'll be leaving in a quarter hour."

Once they were rolling again, the trip leader came back to talk to them, first asking, "All right if I talk to you two together?"

"Yeah. Sure," they answered almost simultaneously.

"OK. So, I'll get through the sensitive stuff first. You`ve read the policy on alcohol, services provided by the nurse and so forth, any questions?"

They shook their heads.

The trip leader continued, "Just to be clear, we do our best with dietary issues but as it says in our literature, religious or strict vegan diets just aren't practical. Any concerns with that?"

"Do you have coffee?" Gus asked.

Baffled, the trip leader replied, "Of course."

"Good, and I guess there'll be a whole lake of fresh water for her," he said, jerking his thumb. Lee thumped him on the shoulder.

"Ow."

The trip leader chuckled and began talking again, "Well, on to the easy part. As I said earlier, we recommend that new acquaintances exchange only first names. I am going to issue you with an ID number which you will use for all identification with the organization for the rest of this trip."

"Seems a bit extreme," Lee said.

"Do you remember a few years ago when an activist was tracked down and harassed in his workplace, until he had to change jobs? Ever since we've used this random number system. Your full actual name will only be used in an emergency. Right. That's everything, unless you have questions." He paused. "No. Good, we'll get into the motel pretty soon."

A couple of hours later the trip leader announced, "OK, we're almost there. Use the numbered ID cards to register. There will be a buffet dinner in the dining room until nine tonight. The bus will leave tomorrow morning at six AM sharp. Wake up call will be five AM." A chorus of groans drowned out his wishes for a good night.

Gus and Lee stuffed the tablet and other oddments into their daypacks. He was leading as they joined the line shuffling towards the front doors. As they got off the bus everybody was milling about in a disorderly process of claiming packs.

Lee's bag was taken off almost immediately but Gus knew his was buried in the back of the cargo hold. He turned to her asking, "Would you like me to get us a room while you watch for my bag?"

Blushing she answered, "I could get my own..."

Now his face coloured, "Sorry, did I misunderstand? If you don't want to share a room with me..."

"Oh. I do, but are you sure? Because that brunette over there is looking at you very hopefully."

"I'm sure." Irritated, he grabbed her ID card telling her, "My pack is a large brown one with no outside pockets." Leaving her to get the packs, Gus stalked toward the motel office. Returning a few minutes later, he saw that Lee was struggling to haul both bags through the loose gravel.

"Here, let me..."

"I can manage," she muttered abruptly. "Go open the door to the room."

Gus held the door and she heaved his bag over the doorjamb then stood outside looking up at him. "Are you sure..."

"What is this? I like you, all right. You're smart. You're beautiful." Pausing he asked, "It isn't your first..."

"No. It isn't. But I'm not beautiful. I have all these freckles. All over. One boy laughed at them."

"Really?" Grabbing her bag, he shoved it into the room. "He's an idiot. Look at you. Your smooth skin, clear blue eyes, this gorgeous cascade of ringlets" He took her hand and pulled her into the room, pushing the door closed behind her.

"More like an eternal tangle." She tipped her head up to kiss him. He gently responded to her touch.

"Also, well, I bulge."

"Where?" he asked. Hesitantly she drew up her t-shirt. He looked down at her bra, which seemed uncomfortably tight. She winced a little before he could get it undone. Feeling her heat on his chest, he leaned into her. Passionately they kissed again as he lifted her onto the bed. Later he came awake with his usual start. Frowning, he stared at his daypack on the other side of the room.

"Relax. We used one of mine," Lee said as she came out of the bathroom.

"Oh good." He added awkwardly, "Not that you could catch anything from me." Lee smiled as she finished drying herself, then slipped into a fresh pair of panties.

He regarded her appreciatively. "I don't see any bulges." Putting her hands under her breasts, she raised them slightly then let them fall.

"Oh." Still feeling awkward he said, "I suppose we missed the buffet."

"Long time ago. However, I've got a bottle of wine I don't want to waste, and Margaret will have packed a major meal."

He sat up abruptly. "Who's Margaret?"

"Margaret is terribly overprotective." Seeing his expression, she laughed then added, "It's OK. I'm twenty. Go shower."

Minutes later he returned rubbing his hair dry to find a spare blanket spread over the bed with cheese, crackers and fruit laid out on top of it. She handed him a motel glass brimming with wine and raised hers. "Here's to good beginnings."

He sipped. "Hmm, I'm already beginning. Would it be insensitive of me to ask you to put on a tee shirt?"

"Not if you put on some shorts." As an afterthought she added, "And a shirt."

They ate quietly for a few minutes before Gus asked, "I don't get why you were so anxious about, you know, uh, before?"

"I've only just started wearing that bra."

"It looks like it kinda hurts."

"It does, but at least I can start a conversation."

"Uh. The 'I'm up here stupid' syndrome."

"Yeah. It's pretty hard to have an intelligent conversation when the boy is drooling at the thought of burying his head in my boobs."

"Speaking of intelligence, you said you were in pre-law. I've never heard of that."

"Not really a program but there are counsellors who will help you choose courses that give you background for the area of law you want to study."

"What would you take to prepare for criminal law?"

"I don't know. I'm prepping for corporate law by majoring in history of government with a minor in environmental studies."

"You know a lot about criminal law though."

"Couple of symposiums. Prep for big protests. I can't demonstrate. Any charge could be used to keep me from being called to the bar. I help represent people who are arrested."

Gus went silent with a pensive expression. Lee reached over the bed and grabbed the corners of the blanket, sweeping up the remains of their meal and depositing it on the floor.

"Fascinating conversation and all but we can have it in daylight."

Stripping her tee shirt up over her head, she climbed onto him and buried her face in his neck. Much later, they crawled under the covers. Later again, they fell into an exhausted sleep.

They were awoken by a loud knock and a cheerful call of, "Good morning. Breakfast in a quarter hour."

"Want first shower?" he asked muzzily.

"No. I need to repack."

A few minutes later he stuck his head out of the bathroom door. "Mind if I grow a beard?"

She stood up so that the morning sun streamed through her glorious hair. Lee shrugged, "I like beards," she said, then went back to packing her bag.

When he came back drying himself, she took one look and said, "Woah. I better get in there quick or we'll miss breakfast for sure."

"Maybe even the bus," he said as she flew past him.

"My bag is packed. You can take it to the bus if you want. I'll meet you in the dining room," Lee called before the shower drowned her out.

Gus was happy to see that her suitcase had somehow lost its wheels and acquired shoulder straps. He picked up both packs and took them to the bus, then went to the dining room. Happily, he loaded up his plate with what he considered a proper breakfast and sat down in the nearly empty dining room. Gradually groups of two or three came in and the room was filled with the quiet buzz of conversation. A silence made Gus look up in time to see Lee coming towards him. She was wearing leggings and a close-fitting top that accentuated what had been hidden the day before. Sliding into the seat opposite him, she sat with a straight-backed posture. Slightly stunned, he gawked at her for a moment then blinked.

"Well, I didn't want any of those booby girls thinking they had a shot."

"Oh, they don't," he said fervently.

"What is that on your plate?"

"Breakfast."

"Bacon, sausage, eggs, hash browns, pancakes with butter and syrup, do you ever eat any fruit?"

"I had orange juice," he said defensively. "Enjoy that yogurt. I bet it's the last one you see for quite a while."

Companionably they finished their meal and went out to the bus. As they boarded, he said, "I looked at the map. There isn't much to see on the way to the camp. If you don't mind, I'm going to take a nap."

"Wouldn't mind taking one myself if there were a quiet corner somewhere."

"Ah ha. I knew my snoring would be an issue." Triumphantly he pulled a mouth guard out of his daypack and put it into his mouth.

"Noo moor shnoorinng." Settling comfortably into the window seat he was soon sleeping with barely a whisper of sound. Smiling, she lifted the centre rest and snuggled up against him. Later they were woken by bouncing and swaying as the touring coach rumbled down a rutted lane into the base camp .

"OK folks. Make sure you take all your stuff with you. Get your packs out from the cargo space. Camp crew will show you where to stack them for now. Quick as you can please, so we can get the bus out of here and keep our costs down. We'll eat in a quarter hour."

As they stepped down, Gus touched her arm. "Our packs are right at the back. Might as well use the washrooms while we wait."

"Good thought."

A few minutes later, he came out of the latrine and saw her walking towards some boats drawn up on a pebbly beach. She ran a hand along the gunnel as she walked along the side of the boat. Reaching inside, she fingered a sail stowed with several long oars. Moving up the other side she bent down to look at the keel then ran her hand down the side of the boat, which had overlapping boards rather like the siding on a house. Gus watched as she looked up at a giant of a man with an unruly head of ginger hair and a beard to match.

"Clinker built," said the giant.

"Amazing. Read about them. Never seen one. Do you build them yourself?"

"No. There's a boat builder in the Indigenous people's village. He and his grandson build them. I go to watch and learn whenever I can."

Lee looked up and saw Gus watching. She slid her palm along the smooth wood of the bow and went to join him.

Chapter Three

A couple of mornings later Gus woke to the cheerful cry of "Let's go. Let's go. We want to be on the water in ten minutes."

"He's kidding right? What about breakfast?" Lee asked.

Rolling out of their sleeping bag, Gus began dressing and said, "No he's serious. Two or three hours of rowing then we pull up on a beach for breakfast. Much easier rowing first thing in the morning while the water is smooth and still."

"Maybe I should have stayed on campus," Lee grumbled, jamming her legs into jeans.

They lugged food packs from the main hall to the beach. The boats were floating sedately in shallow water and the work leader was stowing packs, making sure the long boats were well balanced.

They all gathered round for a cup of coffee and a handful of trail mix as the last volunteers straggled down to the beach. The trip leader called for their attention. "OK folks, I'm passing you over to the work leader now. Have fun. I'll see you in three weeks or so."

"Right, sit on the same oar thwart you had during practice. Quick as you like," said the tall, ginger-haired, broad-shouldered work leader, affectionately known as 'Ginger.' He pushed each of the boats out onto the lake and hopped into the last boat himself. The three boats were soon cutting through the calm of early morning with enthusiastic, if ragged, rowing. Everyone was enthralled by the silent expanse of water just beginning to be tinged with the colours of dawn. A couple of hours later Ginger's boat led to a wide sandy beach. Crew and volunteers quickly heaved the boats onto the sand to make them secure. The steering crew brought food packs and a metal tripod to a circle of stones clearly used as a fire pit for cooking.

"Right, lookout crew will set pegs and tie the boats to the land, then take the volunteers from their boat to gather wood to replace what we use." Anticipating a protest he added, "Dead dry ground wood."

Once the wood was in and everyone had been served hot porridge, Ginger took a cup of coffee and stood looking up the lake. Gus went and stood by him and asked, "Was that a 'pipe'?" Ginger looked at him with a crooked smile. "Like the voyageurs you mean? Nah, that was barely a quarter of the distance they would make before taking a rest stop. Tire you out did it?"

"Well, I won't say it was easy, but it was harder for almost all the others."

"Yeah, wind's freshening in our face too. That will make the rowing harder." Raising his voice, Ginger called, "Time to go folks, finish up. Rinse your dishes. Lookout crew, get the anchor stakes out and stowed with the ropes."

Ginger hustled off to get the food packed up and stowed with the cooking gear. He checked that the fire was completely out, then said, "We'll switch up jobs so you can all learn how to handle this kind of boat." The little flotilla made good progress. By late morning of the next day, everyone could do all the jobs and they were keeping a good pace; when the lookout crew in the lead boat abruptly waved, all the boats turned smoothly into the calm water behind the lee of a point. Volunteers gratefully leaned on their oars or fished cups of water out of the lake.

Stretching the kinks out of his neck, Gus was the first to see the homebound boats. They coasted around a point with their square sails, looking, for all the world, like miniature Viking ships. The crew from the two flotillas exchanged catcalls.

"What, need a rest do you?"

"Careful now, you'll get so sleepy a big wave 'ull cum up an' swamp yee."

Then it was back to the long hard grind of pushing their boats up wind to the next overnight camp. The fit volunteers were getting a second wind but some of the less athletic volunteers fell asleep before supper was cooked.

The next morning, Ginger got them moving early. As they stumbled and grumbled out of their tents and onto the boats, the crew was everywhere helping volunteers to roll sleeping bags and lift packs, giving cheerful words of encouragement.

When boats pulled out, Ginger stood at his place in the lead boat. He twisted to call out, "Right now. Two good pushes and we'll be in the work camp by lunch time."

Gus and Lee were seated mid-boat. She smiled at him, then frowned as the cold damp in the wind bit into the back of her shoulder. Gus raised his eyebrows; she shrugged, murmuring, "Feels like a storm coming."

Later than usual, Ginger broke for breakfast, getting them out of the cold wind by pulling behind another point of land. There was no stack of wood or fire pit, so Gus knew it was not a regular stop. Ginger stood on the beach, needing to shout to be heard over the wind. He called, "Biological break. No fire, cold breakfast, and we are on our way again in a quarter hour."

A few minutes later, Gus held Lee's cup of juice while she retied a bandana over her hair. "Mon Dieu, that is one beautiful head of hair you have," he said.

She snorted, "The way the tangles are tangling into each other I'll have to get it shorn down to half an inch when we get back. It'll look like yours."

Gus eyed the crew who seemed tense, then asked Lee, "What's happening?".

"Rain coming. Maybe a storm," replied Lee. "I guess Ginger wants us in safe harbour before it hits."

"Uh." Gus nodded. "Nothing worse than pitching tents in the rain."

They climbed into their boat and stood ready, with the handles of their oars stuck into the water so they could pole the boat out. Ginger saw them and gave a fractional nod of his head. "OK. Let's go," he called.

Beginning to sense some urgency, everyone got into their place. Soon, with an even more powerful stroke than on the first day, the volunteers created bow waves with their boats. Less than an hour later, the steering crew leaned on the tiller to pull the lead boat in and along closer to the shore. Ginger craned around on his thwart, and then stood up to look over the low headland. The strengthening wind blew his hair back as he squinted up at dark clouds scudding across the sky. Looking back at the crew on the steering oar, Ginger's mouth tightened and the steering crew jerked her head downward.

"Right then," Ginger shouted. "Straight across. Fast as we can."

The steering crews took firm grips on their oars and turned their boats around a headland and into the wind. Ginger's boat led and got upwind, giving the other two boats some shelter. The wind made choppy waves that bounced the boats about. There was a collective grunt as the volunteers reached into themselves and came up with a little more to put into the oars. The waves grew larger as the boats got into open water, making hard work for the crew as the boats climbed up the steep waves, slapped over the peaks and dove down the other side. Sloshing water came in over the bows to soak all the rowers with spray. Suddenly the steep waves levelled out to a long rolling swell and the boats surged ahead.

"That's it," called Ginger. "We're through the worst of it. Just keep the pace and we'll be in soon."

Work camp crew came down to the beach and shoved rollers under the prows of the boats, then held them steady while all the volunteers and crew clambered out.

"All the packs into the mess tent," yelled a sun-bronzed woman, apparently the work camp leader.

Ginger gave the woman a quick hug then said, "Better tip the boats over, eh?"

Nodding, the woman, soon to be known as 'Blondie,' waved in all the crews. The volunteers quickly emptied the lead boat so that the crew could deftly rock it and tip it over. The boat leaned on its side with the keel into the wind.

Gus went to help with the second boat, but the Giant waved him off. "Nah, nah. There's a knack to it and now's not the time to learn. Grab that sledge and drive in pegs. We need to lash the hulls down so the wind doesn't flip them over and wash them away."

By the time everything was secure, the rain was pouring down, driven by violent gusts of wind. Everyone gathered in the mess tent which turned out to be huge, with high screen walls covered by roll down sides. It had distinctly army surplus look to it, as if someone had robbed the set of MASH.

Blondie hopped up on a stool and called out, "Welcome to the work camp. You'll sleep in here for tonight. Find your gear and set up a space for yourself along that wall." She pointed. "Get dry and into a change of clothes. If your gear is wet see me or him." She pointed again, this time at the Ginger. "What is it you've been calling him? Giant? Och, I like tha," she said in a terrible imitation of a Scot's brogue.

Everyone laughed and set to. The afternoon was passed with some orientation talks. The deluge continued, so nobody went out except to scuttle to the latrine and back as quickly as they could. A rib-sticking supper was served with gallons of juice, cocoa and sweet peach cobbler for dessert.

Gus finished his cocoa and looked toward the kitchen area where the sound of washing up could be heard. He glanced at Lee and she nodded, her snarled mess of red hair bobbing wildly. Both were about to get up when Blondie scooped their cups.

"No need. Crew always do kitchen duty the first night. We'll put all of you in the rota tomorrow." She glanced at Lee. "Ah, honey, I could come back in a few minutes and help you to get that hair under control."

"Thanks, I have been dreading trying to do anything with it. Probably be best to get it into a braid."

True to her word, Blondie was back in a few minutes with a stiff bristled brush and began working on Lee's hair. Ginger joined them with fresh mugs of cocoa.

"Have you two done some wilderness travel before?" Ginger asked as he set the mugs on the table and sat down.

"Some canoe tripping but nothing like this," Lee answered.

"Went over the Great Divide once," Gus said.

"Really?" In surprise, Lee jerked her head towards him, wincing as the brush caught in a tangle.

"And back," he added, deadpan.

She laughed and punched his leg but did not move her head this time.

"You two been together long, if you don't mind my asking?" said Blondie.

They were both still for a moment, then Gus answered for them, "Just this trip."

"Really? You've the feel of a pair of old souls," said Ginger.

Taken slightly aback, Gus shifted the conversation by asking, "Think I should get our tent out and hang it to let some of the water drip out overnight?"

"No need," said Ginger. "This storm will have blown out by morning and we'll hang everything out to dry while we do a work session."

Blondie asked, "So what do I call you? Those names on the list are a bit of a mouthful to be shouting out on the water or in the bush."

"The diminutive of mine is 'Gus,'" he said.

Ginger wrinkled his forehead. "How do you get Gus from –? Never mind, Gus works."

Looking at Lee, Ginger began to ask, "What do we call you..."

"Lee!" she said emphatically.

"OK," pronounced Blondie. "Gus 'n Lee it is. Sounds like a pair of comedians." She added, "We usually end up with Blondie and Ginger."

"Don't happen to know what a woodland feline is, do you?" asked Ginger, explaining, "We do crosswords to improve our vocabulary."

"Lynx," suggested Gus.

"Six letters," said Blondie.

"Bobcat," chimed in Lee.

Ginger looked at the page for a moment and exclaimed, "Oh ho. Gus and Lee could be a wonderful resource," as he wrote in the answer.

The four quipped about clues and chatted for a while before Blondie and Ginger pulled on rain gear and went off to their tent. Most of the volunteers were already asleep, not minding the hard, wooden floors. The couple rolled up in their sleeping bags and spooned.

He murmured, "'Night Lee."

"G'night Gussie," she responded, expecting a grunt or a dig in the ribs, but he was already asleep.

As predicted, the next morning dawned sunny with a light breeze. Sleeping bags, tents and wet clothes were sorted and hung out while another immense breakfast was put on the tables.

When the meal had been consumed and the tables cleared, Blondie called, "OK everyone, this morning we are going to show you how we collect and package plastic waste. This afternoon, when everything is dry, you will put up your tents and get settled in."

Being quicker than most of the volunteers, Lee and Gus stood gazing out at the glittering blue water covered by an endless blue sky with a few puffy white clouds drifting across it.

"Doesn't get more beautiful than this," Gus said.

"Nope, Tom Thomson country," Lee replied.

Once the group had gathered, they set off, pushing their way through wild raspberries as they climbed up over a low ridge. Halfway down the other side, back toward the water, the first volunteers stopped abruptly and everyone bunched up around them. There were a few expletives. Before them lay a rocky bay choked with plastic debris. They watched as huge patch of single-use bottles, bags and other rubbish broke loose and flooded into a river at the base of the bay.

Blondie led them the rest of the way down to the shore and turned to face a rather subdued, sober crowd of volunteers. "Upstream from here there is an active and effective program to keep plastic out of the water, all the way to the headwaters of this system. Still, we get this huge glut of garbage where the river flows out of the lake toward the ocean. Hard to imagine the damage we are doing unless you see it." Blondie allowed them a few minutes to take it in.

"Those of us on the crew of Plastic Reuse are thankful for your help. The job for today is to collect large plastic bottles. Later we'll show you how we package them."

After changing into sandals and swimsuits, Ginger and Blondie put on protective gloves, then climbed carefully into the edge of the lake and waded out until they were knee deep in the water. Blondie held open a bag while Ginger pulled large bottles from the bobbing mass of plastic and put them into the bag. Following their example, the volunteers paired up and climbed down into the floating junk.

It did not take long to fill up sixty large bags. Each person took a couple and began trudging back.

As they arrived, Blondie said, "Toss the bags over there by the press."

"What does that thing do?" someone asked.

"Makes bales, demonstration after break," replied Blondie.

After a biological break and making sure everyone was hydrated, the crew gathered with the volunteers around the bale maker. Regarding the contraption, which looked like a large crate bolted onto a heavy timber base, the volunteers speculated about how it worked. The crate stood about four feet high with foot-wide gaps top to bottom on two opposite sides. What looked like a lid lay to one side attached to a peeled log the size of a telephone pole.

"OK," said Blondie. "As you know, there is no effective way to destroy plastic, so we carry as much as possible back out to the base camp and sell it for recycling. A lot of the small trash, like bottle caps or plastic bags, can be packed into recovered bags like ones we used this morning. Obviously, bottles take up a huge amount of space, so this 'press' is used to crush them into manageable 'bales.' It is similar to the presses that fur traders in this area used to bale raw hides for transport down these rivers and across the ocean to European markets.

"We dump the bottles in here, crush them down as small as we can and bind them into bales. You'll take the bales out as cargo in your boats when you return to base camp."

After a demonstration, Blondie lead the volunteers over to a large open tent.

Once everyone had gathered round, a lean muscular young man introduced himself, "I'm the 'general factotum.' Which is to say I can fix most things, and do. Mainly I lead the baling of plastic. First, we have to make string from the large plastic bottles. Gather in and I'll show you how we do it."

Pulling on a pair of heavy work gloves, he picked up a small flat plastic oval. "You're probably all familiar with these. They're the same as the ones used for cutting the corners off milk bags. Cutting a strip should be fairly easy as long as you keep a steady pressure and smooth movement going." Slotting a cutter into a wooden handle, he began to cut a quarter inch wide ribbon off a plastic bottle by going around and around it. "Be careful, the cutters can shatter. Always wear work gloves. The bottles can give you a very nasty version of a paper cut." He had everyone practice for a few minutes.

"Now if you'll move over here, our weaver will show you how to make string out of the ribbons."

"He does love his nicknames," said the smiling woman. "This is very simple really. You just bind the end of three plastic ribbons together and then weave the strands together like a hair braid. About a third of the way down, add in a new ribbon on top of one of the strands, then another third down add in another one and so on." Her gloved hands flew as she demonstrated.

"We need strings about sixteen to twenty feet long to make the baling nets. OK, that's about all I have to say." Smiling again, she looked at the general factotum. "Oh, I should add that I do, actually weave with this stuff. I'm trying to find ways to reuse the plastic ribbons so if you weave or would like to learn, you are welcome to join me."

The volunteers moved over to another corner of the marquee where the general factotum introduced them to a tall redheaded man. "This is Leif, no relation to Eric." The redhead rolled his eyes as one or two people stifled laughs. "We are very fortunate to have him with us because he is one of the few, living souls, who can make a fishing net by hand."

"Yeah, well, you'll get used to his verbosity after a while," said Leif. "This is not really net making, although I can make net, even with vine or other materials you could find in a survival situation. If you're interested, I'd be glad to show you. The plastic string you just learned about is nearly impossible to use for proper net making. It won't hold a knot like a regular cord. We solved this, sort of, by laying out the strings so they form four-inch squares, then we tie off the intersections with recycled plastic string." Leif had been laying and tying a section of net as he spoke. "The string is the only recycled product we have to buy for this project."

"Next the four-by-four or four-by-eight sections are tied together with a running knot. That makes the net bags you saw used in the press. That's about it." Seeing no questions, he said, "General, marshal your troops."

This time nobody tried to suppress their chuckles. The volunteers spread out to the three stations and began learning to reuse plastic bottles.

Over the next few days, everyone settled into a steady rhythm. Hauling plastic into the work camp in the mornings, making nets and packing bales in the afternoons. The pace was steady but not taxing. Plenty of time was spent learning new skills, hiking, fishing or rowing around the area in the mini Viking ships.

Chapter Four

On the last morning, all the volunteers marveled at how quickly the three weeks had passed. Boats were loaded, and the crew were receiving a shower of heartfelt goodbyes and fervent promises to return. With practiced ease the thwarts were filled and better rowing got them to the first camp in late afternoon. Around the campfire, memories were exchanged. Gone were the days of crawling into their sleeping bags at the first opportunity.

On the second day of the return trip, under sail, the boats moved down the lake at a good speed. Their return to the base camp was on schedule to meet the bus, which would ferry them back to their respective lives. Gus lay staring pensively at the billow of the sail. Lee regarded him with concern, then glanced around before she asked, "Care to share?"

He looked at her with an appreciative smile. He also glanced around and since nobody was paying attention to them he spoke softly, "Always wonder what's waiting for me when I get back to civilization."

"Nothing," she assured him. His eyebrows drew into a frown as he regarded her inquiringly. "If you mean about the 'event,'" she continued, "the oil corporation locked down that meeting and wheeled out the PR machine. Getting past their security, the way you did, was embarrassing enough. They don't want any questions asked about their environmental record. You got away clean. Meeting me was a fluke."

"And a very nice fluke at that." His mood seemed to lift a little as he smiled at her. "Yeah, there was no media attention at all. Not a very effective action, really. Next time, I want to draw attention to a corporation's environmental record, I'll need to do it at an event that already has media coverage, preferably live."

"Uh, about that?" She paused hesitantly. He cocked an eyebrow at her, some of the apprehension returning to his expression. "Mmm, do you have any plans?" She stumbled on, "I mean immediate plans, for the next couple of weeks?"

"No, not really, I mean..."

"Would you like to spend them with me? We could, ah..." her invitation petered out.

"Of course, I'd love to spend more time with you. I'd thought about asking you but, " his eyes saddened as he tilted his head down, "well, I have no money so I couldn't take you anywhere."

"Oh. That's all right then. You can come to my family's cottage. I mean my parents will be there and you might have to put up with my oh-so-loathsome little brother, but it'll be fun."

"I thought you were going back to school early, for an environmental seminar."

"I am but that's still two weeks away. What are you going to do next? Ah, uhm, I mean if you don't mind me knowing ..."

"Don't worry. I won't put you in a position where you will be able to tell anybody anything that could cause me problems." In response to her expression, he explained, "I do everything solo and never tell anybody about 'actions.' That way I am less likely to get caught, no offence."

Just then, the lookout in the lead boat gave a shout as that night's campsite came into view. There was a boil of activity as the sail came down; oars went out and short swift strokes brought the boats in to shore. The tents were up, and supper started in no time.

The next day there was less wind and more rowing, but the group got to base camp in time to spend their last afternoon showering, retrieving possessions and getting ready for an early start the next morning. The camp was still outside cell phone range; the evening was passed exchanging contact information and recounting funny exploits for the benefit of the base camp crew. Then decks of cards were brought out for one last game of euchre, or bridge. Others played board games, on actual boards, until people got tired and went to spend the last night in their bedrolls, swearing that was one thing they would not miss.

The next morning, with the last of the rib-sticking breakfasts consumed, they jostled about laughing and talking until just after dawn, when the tour bus pulled into camp. Packs were stowed in the bus's baggage compartment and everyone was in their seat so swiftly that the driver barely had time for a bathroom break.

Once the bus was on the highway, the trip leader stood up and received a round of groans and catcalls. "Now, now," he said good humoredly, "you'll be rid of me soon enough." After people settled down, he continued, "Barring a natural catastrophe, early this evening, we will roll into the same motel as we stayed at on the way up. There will be a couple of breaks today so if you want to be picked up, call on the pay phones or use your cell phones to tell whoever is meeting you. Please return your ID number cards to me either before you leave tonight or after you have registered at the motel. Tomorrow we will make one stop in cottage country. Same deal for people who want to leave us there. For the rest of you, we may be fairly late getting into the city. In the meantime, enjoy your return to junk food, digital communication and hot showers."

At about noon the next day, the bus pulled into a coffee shop beside the highway. The remaining volunteers piled off, laughing and calling to one another, as they set out in search of washrooms, coffee and the other amenities of civilization.

Gus pulled Lee's pack out from under the bus then got his own. They hitched them onto their shoulders and looked around. He was about to ask, when Lee jerked up her chin and said, "Here they are." A top-of-the-line, off-road SUV pulled into the parking lot.

The rather gangly youth who climbed out of the passenger seat looked around belligerently. Meanwhile the driver in a black shirt and slacks came around to hand down a slim, middle-aged woman in a

KILLING OUR GRANDCHILDREN

brightly flowered sundress, who took one look at Lee and exclaimed, "Darling, whatever has happened to your hair?"

"Hello Mother," Lee said as they went into the routine of air kissing on both cheeks.

"Never mind dear, there is a very good stylist here in town. Not as good as Alfredo's, of course, but we'll get your hair put to rights."

"I don't really want to spend my holiday time in a salon. I'm sure I'll be able to make it presentable with conditioner and a hair dryer."

Gus stood to one side observing this exchange, somewhat nonplussed. When Lee's mother turned to him, he proffered his hand, saying politely, "Pleased to meet you, people call me Gus." Lee's mother barely touched his hand in response, replying in a stiff voice, "Charlotte, and this is my son Leo." As he shook Leo's hand, Charlotte turned back to Lee exclaiming, "Oh, darling let me see your hands. Surely, they're not rough and dirty like his. Really, we must get you a manicure, at once."

Rolling her eyes, Lee said emphatically, "No, we must go to the cottage and enjoy ourselves." Hitching up her pack Lee waved away the driver saying, "I've got it Jimmy, just open the hatch please." Gus followed her to the back of the SUV where she turned and took his pack from him mouthing "It'll be OK."

They all climbed in and seated themselves on luxurious leather seats. "So, Sis, this is the new flame huh? Looks a little rough around the edges," said Leo.

Lee brandished a fist at him and said, "Watch it, I have all these new muscles that I would just love to exercise."

"Children please. This is the young man who was at the, uh, camp, with you dear?"

"Yes Mother. Gus and I have been together since the beginning of the trip."

"Well, I had Margaret air out the guest lodge and of course your room in the main cottage has been prepared."

"That's nice but I'll be staying in the guest lodge."

"Oh boy, Sis. Dad's going to love this."

Lee ignored him and glared at her mother until the older woman turned away. For the rest of the drive Charlotte silently stared out the window, while Lee chattered to Gus, pointing out the landmarks of her childhood. Jimmy turned into a long downhill driveway and pulled up beside what looked to Gus like a small house. Lee got out and said, "We'll see you at dinner."

Her mother asked, "Can I send Margaret to help with your hair? Perhaps you'd like some of your clothes."

"Yes, that would be nice Mother. Margaret will know what to bring." She slid the side door shut and went around the back of the vehicle. With a wink, Jimmy handed them their packs.

Running his fingers over a log wall, Gus stepped inside the guest lodge and paused to look in wonder at a huge fieldstone fireplace. "You must be rich as Croesus. Are you sure you want me here?"

"Jimmy will have the sense to warn Margaret." She grabbed his hand and dragged him into the bedroom. "We have at least an hour of privacy." Pulling off his shirt she pushed him onto the bed then climbed on top of him. In a while she rolled onto her side. Regarding him intently she said, "Reality check. I'm the same person as I was this morning."

"You are." Apprehensively he added, "But your family?"

"Go shower. Margaret will be bringing you some clothes so you can dress for dinner."

"You dress for dinner?" he stared at her askance.

"No. Well, yes. Just khaki pants and polo shirts though."

A short while later, wrapped in a towel, he stepped out of the bathroom and came face to face with a pleasant-looking middle-aged woman. "Excuse me." He looked around wondering what to do.

"There should be bathrobes on the back of the door, sir."

"They're monogramed, can anyone use them?"

"Yes sir. I have laid out a selection of clothes for you in the front bedroom."

"Here's the last of it," Lee said as she came in and dumped an armload of laundry into a hamper by the woman's feet. "Hey, I see you've met Margaret. Go dress. There are books and a computer in the room beyond the fireplace. This is going to take awhile," she added, pulling up a handful of her hair.

Later as they walked down a steep path towards an even larger house, he suggested, only half joking, "So I should just use the same fork that you do, I guess."

"Don't be silly. The servants will bring out the correct cutlery with each course." Looking up she saw his expression and hastened to add, "Not really, it's no worse than eating in a restaurant."

Lee led him onto a deck looking out over the sparkling lake. Below them, a sleek cedar strip motorboat was moored to a dock cluttered with water skis, canoes, kayaks and lounge chairs. An imposing man turned from the railing to regard his daughter.

"Hello Daddy," said Lee, stretching up to kiss him on the cheek. "This is Gus."

Impassively Lee's father asked, "Well young man. What will you have to drink?"

Nervously Lee interjected, "Do you have any of the new lager from our craft brewery?"

The tall man with a mane of silver hair closed his eyes fractionally as he looked down at his daughter. "Yes, I believe we do."

"Oh good, we'll have a couple of those."

"So, my dear, how long will your friend be staying?" inquired Lee's mother.

"We've both got a couple of weeks of holiday."

"How nice. Perhaps your father could take you on his famous round the lake tour tomorrow."

"Afraid not, my dear. The problem I mentioned yesterday has been confirmed, as I expected. I'll be going back to the city after dinner."

There was some stilted conversation, then they were ushered into a dining room with floor to ceiling windows and seated on one side of an oval table which allowed all of them to enjoy the view.

"What a wonderful table. I don`t believe I`ve ever seen one like it," commented Gus politely.

"I should hope not. It's unique and it cost me a pretty penny," responded Leo.

"Beautiful wood," said Gus. "Mahogany?"

"Yes," said Leo. "I just came back from our holdings in Brazil. That is where this wood came from. You can tell by the distinctive colour."

"You're back early aren't you?" Lee asked.

"Yes. Father got me into the Dutch civil engineering school. It's only a year but the program starts next week."

"Is that the course that specializes in flood control?" Gus asked.

"That's right. We have shorefront land in Florida. I'm going to oversee projects in the water containment division which our construction company is developing."

"Leo, you will be learning from an engineer with thirty years of experience." Lee's father gave his son a stern look then turned to Gus and continued, "A huge demand for shorefront water management is expected in coming years. Should be very profitable. What do you do young man?"

"Construction mostly, I expect to be going to school next month."

"Really?" Lee asked in a surprised tone. "What school are you going to?"

"Not one you're likely to recognize." His crooked smile was followed by a wink. "I'm going to get my heavy operator's ticket."

"But that's..." Leo's voice trailed off.

"Manual labour? Not quite. Using a backhoe is easier than digging a ditch with a pick and shovel," Gus replied with a widening smile.

"Once I'm qualified, I'll be working to relocate coastal farming communities to higher ground so they can avoid flooding."

"Why would they build their houses too close to the water's edge in the first place?"

Gus regarded the younger man for a moment then explained, "The next community I'll be helping has been on its island for over a hundred years."

"Why not put berms around it?"

"Sea levels are rising too fast and flooding is unpredictable. You can get dikes built and the next year the water just surges right over them."

"Yes," Lee's father nodded, "very likely a growing demand over the next few decades. A company entering that market now would be well positioned to expand."

"Company? Oh, no sir. An organization called Rising Oceans will provide the machinery and funding. I work for room and board."

The older man gave Gus a contemptuous look and asked, "And how will you support a family?" Gus shifted uncomfortably in his chair turning toward Lee. With her lips pressed together in an obvious effort to prevent herself from butting in, Lee nodded to Gus. He continued, "Well sir, my immediate goal is to help keep the world habitable. In ten years, if I think my children will be able to thrive or at least survive on the earth, I will give some thought to settling down and raising a family."

"Are you sure the planet can afford to have you take two weeks off?" asked Lee's father, raising an eyebrow.

"It certainly can," Lee burst out. "We want to swim, laze around in the sun, canoe up to 'kids beach'..."

Leo interjected, "Water ski, roar down to Annie's place..."

"You know perfectly well I haven't water skied in years," snapped Lee, giving her brother a ferocious look. "We'll stick with the non-polluting sports, thank you."

As if on cue, they heard a faint buzzing sound.

"That will be the plane," said Lee's father rising from the table. He paused and gave Lee an intense glare. "You are still going to law school?"

"Yes Daddy." Smoothly she added, "To study corporate law."

Lee took Gus's arm and they all trooped down to the dock where the pontoon plane was gliding to a halt. Her father clambered aboard, and they watched as it taxied downwind to get into the best takeoff position.

Lee's mother wrung her hands saying, "I wish he'd use a helicopter."

"It takes an experienced pilot to get a seaplane off in this bay," explained Leo. "The plane needs to climb fast to clear the hills safely."

Seeking to distract Lee's mother, Gus pointed at a sailboat bobbing on its buoy as the seaplane passed it. "Is that a Y Fourteen?"

"Why yes," her mother said. "Do you sail?"

"Not much, what little I've done was on oceans."

"We have an O Twenty-Four on the south shore. It can really go, provided the crew scrub down the hull regularly. Ocean scum is becoming a real nuisance," put in Leo.

Just then, the engine ran up to a roar, driving the plane along the water to claw up over a hilly shore.

"I need a drink," said Lee's mother turning toward the house with her hand on Leo's arm.

Gus and Lee stood watching the plane's wake wash ashore until the lake became quiet and still, reflecting the sunset's colours.

Frowning, Gus began to ask, "How do you ..." Seeing Lee's brows draw together he stopped talking.

Adroitly Lee kept the conversation going by remarking, "The lake isn't like an ocean with its constant gurgle of sound, is it?"

His face smoothed as he caught her warning and changed his question so that it became innocent. "How do you get to Annie's?"

"We go out to the narrow dogleg channel – in the mornings, the wind will just blow us down into the main lake. The difficult part is getting home if the breeze is blowing in your face. We have to tack back and forth like mad to get back up the channel."

"You steer then. I'll handle the front sail." Her smile widened.

They turned to watch the sunset's oranges become crimson, then purple, as darkness settled.

Chapter Five

Lee led him up a different path towards the guest lodge. "That heavy machinery school you're going to. Is that the one inland from the western seaboard's main port?"

He gave her a startled look. "Surprised you know of it."

"Remember those operators who refused to bulldoze in a toxic waste site?" Gus nodded, so she continued, "They trained there. Eco Law Clinic defended them. That's where I volunteer. We used the code of ethics they had been taught in their defence."

"Didn't get them off though, did it?" said Gus in a slightly bitter tone.

Lee acknowledged ruefully, "No. But it did keep them out of jail." She led him to a lookout point and turned to watch the rising moon.

"Uh oh. You can't be out of breath," he began to tease, but seeing her serious expression, fell silent.

"That's where I'm studying law. The port university teaches a very strong climate protection curriculum."

"Does your father approve of that?"

"Just now I'm using the 'what he doesn't know won't hurt him' tactic. After that, I'll see how far I can get with a 'know thy enemy' defence by pretending I only want to be able to help protect his companies. Anyway, the thing is..." She paused in an uncharacteristically hesitant manner.

He helped her out by saying, "If you would like to keep seeing me, that's good because I'd like to keep seeing you."

Relieved Lee said, "Actually I have a house off campus. Nobody is sharing it with me. Or has even spent the night, for that matter." Looking up apprehensively she continued, "Seems when your name is on a building..." She shrugged.

"I can see where that would be intimidating."

"The law library, no less. It was my father's uncle who donated the money. That doesn't seem to make much difference. So, what do you think?"

Uncertainly he asked, "About?"

"Living with me, or having a room in my house, or staying on weekends?" Her voice petered out. "Oh, you don't want to," she said in a crestfallen voice.

"I do. Really I do but..." He fell silent, leaning forward on the lookout railing.

"I know it's a long way from the port to the school..."

He shook his head. "It isn't that."

She rattled on, "I've got an electric car. You could drive it to your machinery school, no problem."

"No need. It's only about ten miles inland to the school. It's in the valley, flat, I already cycled it a couple of times. That's not the problem..."

"It's me. I know I'm not really very good looking. I thought the sex was OK. Wasn't it? Is it too soon to suggest living together? I know I can be brash. Growing up entitled makes me feel..."

"It isn't any of that stuff," he said, slightly impatient.

"It's my family. I knew it. They're such arrogant self-centered capitalist oligarchs that they think climate change is a hoax designed to foment a socialist revolution."

"It's none of those things. Would you stop talking for a minute?" She stopped. Frowning he stared out over the water for a while. "Thanks. See I've been thinking about this. I wanted to invite you to live with me. I didn't, obviously. Partly owing to money. I don't have any and I won't earn much."

"That doesn't matter. Embarrassingly, I have way more than I need. It's in a trust too, so my father can't get at it. I can finance anything we want to do."

"Jeez will you stop talking?"

"What's the problem then?" Gus looked at her, pursing his lips and spreading his hands. "Sorry," she said and stopped talking.

"Hypothetically, OK?" Lee nodded. Gus continued, "You can deny this conversation ever occurred if you need to. Wait, nobody can hear us right?"

"No. That's why I brought us up here. I think my father made this lookout a dead zone so he could talk business here."

"Sheesh. Problem is if I let something slip, talked in my sleep, got drunk, high or just ran off at the mouth, then you might know something that needed to be kept secret."

"I see what you mean. At least, it would be an ethical issue. I could be accused of failing to act as an officer of the court. After that my membership in the bar association could be taken away so I wouldn't be able to practice law." She mused for a moment then added, "If we were married I couldn't be compelled in court."

"Getting married might be a bit extreme, I do snore after all."

"I'd have to research what protection we could get from a common-law relationship." Belatedly she registered his attempt to lighten the mood and gave a little laugh, then completed her thought, "Two years before common-law would be any help to us."

"That's not the worst of it though. I will keep things to myself. It is the only way to stay safe. Trouble is I've only had a couple of relationships and those have been short. I have never been with anyone while I was planning an action or waiting to see if I had gotten away with it."

"Except this time," she said with a smile.

"When I'm getting ready for an action I get closed up, anxious, even paranoid. I don't want to be like that with you..." He looked distressed. "Plus, I could be gone for chunks of time. A month, two, I can't predict how long."

"Do that before exams, would you? That's when I need the fewest distractions."

This time it was Gus who missed the humour. "Sooner or later, I'll get caught. No control over what happens then. I could get sent to prison for a long time."

"Or you could be celebrated as a conscientious climate activist."

Gus sighed, "I love spending time with you. It just seems wrong to put you at risk."

"I hadn't thought that deeply about 'risks.' In fact, I had pretty much forgotten how we first met. Odd that every time I think of those oil executives with green goo running down their faces it cracks me up, but it doesn't remind me of you."

He took her hand and they turned toward the lodge.

"We can talk some more and make a decision later in the week. In the meantime, I really want to try out that Y Fourteen. I've never sailed on fresh water before. The waves are so small. Do the winds bounce off the hills?"

A few days later, in beautiful sunshine with a breeze in their faces, they were sailing back after a pleasant day visiting with Lee's friends at Annie's cottage. She turned the boat and he clambered over the centreboard and pulled the rope attached to the front sail behind him. "It wasn't so hard, sailing back, against the wind," he said smiling at her.

"Mostly because of your work with the jib. Without it the only way we could have gotten up this cursed dogleg channel would have been to get out and walk the boat along in the shallows."

"Ah, the loathsome brother would have loved that."

"Uh. Now that you've had a full week's worth of him, I'll have no hope of getting you to see me again, much less live with me."

"Mmm. I'm still stuck in the same place with that. How about you?"

A mast stay thrummed a little. Lee listened to the whistling of the wind for a moment then adjusted course. "Well, once I'm a lawyer, you can hire me, then we would be protected by 'client attorney privilege.' In the meantime, I think you're worth the risk."

"Huh. But you wouldn't be immune to the risk."

"No. If I knew something I didn't want to admit to publicly, I'd just lie. My father would either buy me out of it or his lawyers would get me treated like a spoiled love-addled child."

"Speaking of spoiled, what is your brother..." The roar of the motorboat surging towards the sailboat cut him off.

"Into irons," she yelled, turning the sailboat into the wind. Gus looked at her in shock. "Get in the middle, sit there and don't move. Pull the rope loose so that the front sail flaps," she ordered. As he struggled to obey, the motorboat bore down on them.

"Get ready to pull on the right-hand rope but stay sitting there."

The speedboat blasted past pushing a huge wake towards them. "Now," she commanded. Then she yelled, "Your other right." The sailboat rocked dangerously and water slopped in soaking both of them. Squinting at the sail and the waves ahead, Lee asked, "What is he doing now?"

Gus, who could see the motorboat over her shoulder, said, "Looks like he's stopped; or is he turning?"

"Uh. Makes bigger, rougher waves that way. Get ready to go into irons..." Seeing his look of uncertainty, she explained, "I'll turn, you stay where you are and let the sail flap." She cocked her head listening for the motorboat. As Leo roared by again, she swiftly turned the boat. He obeyed her orders, letting the rope loose so that the front sail flapped.

When Lee had gotten them moving again, Gus said, "This seems dangerous. Why is he doing it?"

"Trying to dump us," she spoke in a sharp breathless voice, watching her brother's boat turning around. "His favorite trick since he was seven; here he comes again."

Once the motorboat had passed, she got them sailing again. "He was always a brat. This though," she shook her head, "you're right, it's dangerous."

They rode down a wave made by the motorboat. Lee brought the sailboat back on course for the dock while Gus crouched over the centreboard.

"What's he doing?"

"Don't see him. There's a wake trail into the channel though."

"OK. Set the jib, pull the front sail in tight. Don't tie it off, keep holding the rope in your hand. Let me know as soon as you see him coming towards us." She worked furiously to keep the sailboat going as fast as possible.

"Here he comes again."

She took a quick look over her shoulder. "I'll need you to catch hold of the white buoy floating near the dock so we can tie up. There should be a grappling hook in the foredeck locker." Catching herself, she explained, "A big hook in that cupboard up front."

Keeping the rope tight so the wind would blow into the front sail, he slid forward, searching for the hook. "Don't see any hook," he called.

"Little turd took it out." She snatched a glance over her shoulder. The motorboat was gaining fast. The buoy was close, but she had no room to maneuver.

Gus grabbed a rope tied to the front of boat yelling, "I'm going to give you a countdown. When I say 'now,' stop the boat, into irons, or whatever." With no time for discussion, he began a count, shouting to be heard over the roar of the approaching engine. "Ready." A second count of "Steady." He raised his arm, afraid she would not hear him, then chopped his hand down as he shouted, "Now." Clamping his teeth around the bow rope, he dove over the side. Two swift underwater strokes took him to the buoy chain. Wrapping the bow rope around the chain, he hastily tied a knot then swarmed up onto the Y Fourteen's bow to take down the front sail. Lee had already lowered the main sail.

Leo's voice rang out over the water, "Almost got you that time, Sis."

Jimmy, who had witnessed the entire incident from the dock called out, "Are you all right, miss?"

"Fine Jimmy, thank you. The grappling hook is not on board, see if you can find it, would you?"

"Tie this up first," her brother ordered, tossing Jimmy the painter from the motorboat.

Lee and Gus stowed gear and reefed down the main sail. Jimmy came to the end of the dock with the hook in hand.

"Where was it?"

"Under the ski ropes, miss, same as always. Although it has been years since I needed to search for it."

She swam in, took the hook and swam back, giving it to Gus to put back in its proper place on the sailboat. Gus hopped into the water beside her and they swam in together. The pair climbed up onto the dock taking towels from Jimmy. "That was very bravely done, sir. No rope burns or scrapes, I hope."

Drying her hair Lee said, "I have a friend who held a mainsail line in her mouth like that. There was a gust and she lost both her eye teeth."

He squinted at her through water drops and asked, "Wasn't there an under sixteen international sailboat final where that happened?"

"Yes, that's the one."

"Hey. Her crew had red hair."

Lee blushed. "We managed a Silver."

After a nap and 'dressing' for dinner, they walked down the path toward the main house. Thoughtfully he asked her, "Does your brother often do things like that?"

"Yes, for as long as I can remember. He'll get involved in any foolhardy escapade if he gets a kick out of it."

Absorbing that statement, Gus nodded slightly, as if something fitted into place. She was beginning to recognize the phases of his thinking, so she walked on quietly, waiting for him to speak.

"That motorboat stunt, it seemed, I don't know. Personal? Vindictive?"

"Oh, it's always personal with him, he's been coming after me like that for as long as I can remember. No reason, just because. If you were the son of a company's partner or a stockholder, though, that would be business. He would be courteous, helpful and perhaps even supportive."

"Will he really take control of the family fortune?"

"Probably. I have an older brother. He's brilliant, in an academic way, not the unfeeling 'cut-throat' kind of personality my father decrees is necessary for business."

"Where does that leave you?"

"Oh, I'll be alright. My grandmother could see how the family power dynamic would work out. She set up a trust for each of us with the investments spread over all the family businesses and into a wide variety of other companies. That way whoever took control of the family 'fortune' would hurt themselves if they tried to tamper with the trusts of the other two."

As they stepped onto the wide deck in front of the living room, her mother said, "Oh, there you are dear. We have just enough time for a drink before dinner."

"I'll have another of those craft lagers," Gus said. "What would you like, honey?"

Blinking at his first ever use of a diminutive, Lee hesitated, then asked, "Is there any Riesling? If not, any dry white wine will be fine."

"I'm sure there is," said her mother, looking pointedly at her son.

There was an awkward pause, which Gus covered by saying, "I know where the drink cabinet is."

Returning a few minutes later he overheard a hissed "...childish stunt," which seemed to be the end of Lee's stinging condemnation. Handing her a glass of wine, Gus turned to Leo, with a bland expression, and said, "You were saying, that you would be working with your father's flood management division. Do you have any other businesses that deal with climate change issues? Electric cars for instance?"

"Only if we can see a way to make a profit," replied her brother. "Electric cars are unproven. The batteries are a problem. It may be possible to make them commercially viable in urban environments, but they will never be effective for long haul transportation of goods."

"Really? I thought there was a company producing an electric truck."

Lee gave Gus a 'what are you doing?' look, as they went into the dining room. Her brother, oblivious to his audience, began a long lecture on the profits to be made from catering to what he called the 'green goofs.' Whenever he began to wind down, Gus set him off again with another question. Lee's mother seemed relieved to be having a conversation without conflict and maintained an appearance of polite interest. Adopting an attentive expression, Lee demurely listened while enjoying the meal.

Once they were safely on their way to the lodge, Lee asked, "What was that all about?"

With a crooked smile and a glint in his eye, Gus replied, "Always good to know what the enemy is thinking." Glancing quickly around he added, "You never know what some activist might target next."

"Well, I think laws and enforcement are the way to go."

"Umm. Five years of university and two years of articling before you can start on that. No offence, honey, but I think we'll be crispy critters before the law can rein in the corporations."

"Hey, you called me 'honey' again."

"Sorry, didn't mean to demean you. I said that in front of your brother so he would think I'm the same kind of bigoted chauvinist he is."

"I'm not offended, sweetie."

"Thank goodness," he said. "I was afraid you wouldn't want me anymore. Is your offer still open?"

Throwing her arms around him, she gave him a huge hug. "Of course it is, if you can stand to live with such a heel-dragging, law-bound activist as myself."

"I think I can manage, even though it is rather like fiddling while the globe burns."

Two days later, they stood on a railway platform, waiting while a locomotive was hooked to their railway cars. Lee's mother took an enormous food hamper from Margaret and thrust it into Gus's hands.

"Really Mother, there is a dining car."

Her mother sniffed, "When I was a child, dining car food was worse than aeroplane food. Really, in this day and age, whoever heard of taking a four-day train trip when a plane can get you there in three hours? You could starve before you get there. Why do you have to go to university all the way out there on the west coast, anyway?"

Ignoring the university question, Lee said, "Tourists enjoy seeing the country. There will be much less pollution this way, if regular travelers make it a viable service."

Mercifully, the conversation was ended by the conductor calling, "All aboard, that's getting aboard."

"Safe trip darling." Unable to evade her mother's farewell rituals, Lee waved goodbye to Margaret and Jimmy.

In their compartment was a vase of fresh cut flowers with a card. Reading the handwritten note from the railway's president, Gus thought, 'I could get seduced by this life of luxury.'

Chapter Six

Lee paid off the taxi, while Gus got their packs from the trunk. She grabbed her mother's hamper, still half-full of non-perishable food.

"Never ridden in one of those electric taxi cabs before," said Gus.

"Not many of them. That's why we had to wait so long at the train station. Usually I book ahead," said Lee.

Gus's attention shifted from Lee to looking at the beautiful old house. Lee fumbled with her keys and let them in. Opening a front hall closet she punched in an alarm cancelling code, telling him apologetically, "I have to. Some of the artwork is very valuable."

"Lovely flowers, fresh cut too," he replied indicating a crystal vase.

Taking her pack, she led him up the stairs explaining as she went, "I've a classmate, Amy, a friend really, who looks after the house when I'm away. She cleans while I'm here. I pay her well, because I can, so she doesn't have to tend bar. This way she has time to study and such. When she gets arrested for protesting it can be a bit of nuisance but otherwise it works well for both of us."

Shepherding Gus into a bedroom at the back of the house, she flicked on the lights and turned to look, apprehensively, at his expression. He gazed around at the huge room with an ensuite bathroom, a wall of built-in closets, and then walked to the windows. Running his finger along a seam, he said, "These are leaded windows."

"Yes, original. My grandfather had the house built for my grandmother and he brought her here as a bride. This was her home for the rest of her life. I'm glad she left it to me. I truly love every inch of it."

"That can't have pleased your brothers."

"She left my older brother the ranch which makes him as happy as this house makes me. The loathsome lad got a huge tract of land. He's trying to find oil on it."

"There's an old man in your yard," he told her with a note of concern in his voice.

She moved to stand beside him. "Oh, that's George. My father pays him to keep an eye on me. We have an understanding. I let him look after the outside of the house, but he never gets to come inside to do his spying. He was my hire originally because he really does keep a magnificent garden but he just couldn't resist my father's pressure, few people can."

"I don't expect he likes using all these new-fangled, ecologically friendly products."

"No, but he does use them. Come and look at the other rooms."

Midway to the front of the house, she passed two doors. "Guest room on the right, bathroom on the left. In a rush we can both shower at once." Swallowing nervously she led him to a pair of doors at the front of the hall. The one on the left was set in the wall at an angle. She opened it. "This is my workroom and this," she went on, opening the door on the right, "can be yours or if you prefer your own bedroom..." Her voice trailed off.

"I'm happy to make a bedroom for myself in here." At her downcast look he added with a twinkle in his eye, "Your room is rather cramped."

She swatted him on the ear. "Urrh, sometimes you are not funny." She stretched up to kiss him, then clasping his hand said, "Come on, let's see what Amy has put in the fridge. Later I'll clear out some closets for you."

"Um. I think half of one will be enough."

"Oh no. I want an entirely separate one for all your filthy, sweaty, work clothes."

They spent the rest of the day settling in. He explored the nooks and crannies of the house while Lee cleared space in closets and cabinets, put out fresh towels and did her best to make the house a welcoming for Gus. Climbing into bed that night, she looked at him reclining on the pillows with a book in hand." Will you have any furniture you want to bring?"

He looked at her askance. "Tomorrow I'll go and collect my bike. I have a trailer for it that'll hold all my stuff."

"I usually take public transit, but we can take the electric car in the morning and I'll drop you off before class."

"No. I'll go alone. That will keep it private."

"Oh. Private. Right. What I don't know, I can't tell. I'd forgotten. We'll need to buy you a proper desk."

"What?" Again, he looked at her in astonishment. "Give up that solid oak, turn-of-the-century roll top? Are you kidding?"

"The drawers are broken. The slats are warped, and the side is sun-scorched. I had it appraised. It's not worth fixing."

"Fixing. Ha, I've a friend who is a cabinetmaker. We'll restore it to its original condition."

She smiled at him. "You have a friend? That I can meet?"

"Harrumph," he chuckled. "We'll have to smuggle him in when George isn't here."

Laughing, Lee clicked out the lights with a remote.

"Oh dear, I've descended into slothful decadence."

"Not just yet," she replied, tugging at his tee shirt.

The next morning, he sleepily bumped into the food hamper where Lee had dumped it on the stairs. She came flying along the hallway, travelling mug in one hand saying, "I'm late. Oh, I forgot about the hamper. I can't manage it with this bag."

He regarded the huge book bag she had over her shoulder. "How can you be late? It's only five thirty."

"Seven o'clock class. Public transport is slow, even at this time of the morning."

"There's a food bank I can stop at. Where do you keep bags?"

"Under the—wait, what do you need a bag for?"

"I won't have room to bring the hamper back with me."

"Oh, just give them the hamper as well. My mother won't expect to see it again." Scooping her keys from the side table she rushed out the door.

Slightly dazed, Gus bent and picked a can out of the hamper. "Pâté de Foie Gras," he read from the label. "Hope it doesn't make somebody sick."

The door smashed open and Lee flew in. "I did this wrong." Planting a big kiss on his lips she said, "I'll be back around five," and flew out the door again. Bemused Gus gently closed the door behind her.

That evening she arrived home at six thirty. "Sorry, sorry."

"No worries," he said handing her a glass of wine. "I made a salad with cold cuts."

She looked at him, wide eyed, then took a gulp of wine. "Really? I've been worrying about what to cook for the last half hour."

"Problem solved," he said, setting bowls of salad, condiments, pickles and plates of meat and cheese on the table.

She sank into the chair he pulled out and took a slice of bread. "Umm, I love fresh baked bread with butter."

"I hope it's OK, eating in the kitchen. That dining room table looks like antique cherry."

"Hmm, yes. Came from England, I think," she said around a mouthful of bread and cheese. "Oh, yes, I'm supposed to ask you, 'How did your day go?'"

"You are 'supposed' to ask me?"

"Yes." She stopped eating. "I've never been in a real relationship before, so I was reading an advice column on the bus. It said..."

"Ah. Well, my day went marvellously. I got my stuff. Ben can't come this weekend, but he thinks he can come next Saturday. My school was annoyed that I skipped the first day but didn't throw me out. That's about it. How was your day, 'dear'?"

She looked at him, swallowed, and then asked, "Are you making fun of me?"

"Sort of, I guess. We've been together what, six weeks? We seem to be doing just fine making it up as we go along."

She looked at her plate for a moment. "Column was written by some ninety-year-old woman who is probably a man anyway, so don't know how good the advice is. It also said I should cook dinner and that would have been a total disaster."

"What do you usually do on the bus?"

"Study."

"Why don't you stick to that and I'll cook whenever I can."

"I never eat in the dining room. I'm terrified of breaking the china. Usually, I just pour some wine, make up a bowl of something and shovel it in while I watch online news in my workroom."

"As amazing as this may sound, I may civilize you slightly by expecting you to join me for dinner, even if it is at the kitchen table."

"Sounds good." She frowned slightly. "But when am I going to fit in watching the news?"

The next evening, Lee came through the door shaking rain off her clothes. "Mmm. That smells good."

"Meat stew and mashed potatoes. The ride home was pretty wet and cold so I thought you might want something hot."

"Why don't you sit here?" he said, putting a bowl down at the middle seat in front of the laptop. "You might want to put a password on your Wi-Fi, but in the meantime I've been streaming the public television station. Gives the most balanced news coverage, I think. If you're late you can skip back to the beginning and get the news summary."

After a while, she muted the sound on a book review and asked him, "How's your ride?"

"Not bad. Like I said, mostly flat. Going out of town when most of the traffic is coming in and vice versa. I'll need to leave about the same time as you to give me a cushion in case there's a holdup on the road."

"Won't that be a problem if your classes go late?"

He gave a short chuckle. "No late classes, honey. This is a union shop. Starts at seven, two fifteen-minute breaks, an hour for lunch and we're done at four."

"You leave the unpaid overtime to we effete, salaried suckers, eh?"

"Got that right. Another beer?"

"Sure," she said absentmindedly as she turned up the sound to listen to an update on a current court case.

So, they settled into a harmonious routine. He cooked. They ate together most evenings. She read constantly. He fixed squeaky hinges and dripping faucets. Friday evening a couple of weeks later, as they started to watch a movie, Gus told her, "Ben's coming tomorrow."

"Tomorrow? Wait, you said the weekend after next."

"That was the week before last," he said with a smile.

"Oh, I really want to meet him. I forgot to tell you; I'm doing legal assistance at the protest tomorrow." Frowning she added, "Supposed to be there all day. The police won't start detaining people until the afternoon but the organizers like us to be there first thing and get introduced, so people will recognize us. That way the protesters will see a friendly face in the police station." Gloomily she added, "I'm not really needed in the morning. The high profile 'pro bono' guy does the 'what to do if you are taken into custody' speech."

"Couldn't you get them to wave a placard with your face on it or something?"

"I don't like to be a prima donna. Hmm. Pause that will you?" Grabbing her phone, she left the rec room. A few minutes later, she came back. "All set."

"That's unfortunate. Ben just called to say he couldn't make it."

She stared then gave him her squint-eyed look. "You don't even have a phone."

"Busted."

They settled in to enjoy the movie with a bottle of wine. The next morning, the doorbell was ringing as Lee came downstairs pulling her hair into a ponytail. Gus yelled from the kitchen, "It's not locked. Come in."

Lee found herself on the landing looking down at a man who had a cheerful smile. "You must be Ben."

"I am. You would be the lady of this magnificent house," Ben said appreciatively, looking around at the carved woodwork. Just then, the door behind him burst open, bouncing off him and back into a tall lithe woman, knocking grocery bags from her hands. Bottles flew into the air landing with a crash, a pasta bag split and fruit rolled everywhere.

"Ah! I so wanted to make a good impression on your beau," groaned the new arrival. "I'm Amy," she said to the laughing Ben. "I'm not usually so clumsy."

Gus looked down the hall from the kitchen. Biting his tongue so as not to laugh, he collected a brush, dustpan and cleaning rags before coming into the front hall. By that time names had been sorted out. Ben turned to him, saying, with a smirk on this face, "May I introduce you to your housekeeper, Amy."

"For that you may help her clean up while I prevent the bacon from burning. Lee, please come and see to the coffee?"

Ben opened his mouth to make a remark, but thought better of it and turned to help Amy. Later as they sipped their coffee and nibbled tasty bits of food, Gus looked at the stacks of groceries. Turning to Amy, he observed, "You must think me a terrible glutton."

"I didn't know what to get. Lee's perfectly happy if I leave five pre-packaged salads, two frozen dinners and a couple of bottles of wine, provided I make sure the coffee jar is full. You work outdoors. I thought you might have a 'steak and potatoes' kind of appetite."

"He likes his steak, fresh and bloody," Lee put in with a wink.

Taking her seriously, Amy replied, "There's a wonderful butcher just around the corner."

"I'm rarely here when they're open," responded Gus. "Could you get some meat that will keep in the freezer? Stewing beef, lean ground chuck, soup bones, stuff like that."

"Sure," said Amy looking troubled.

"It's all right Amy. I still need you to look after things. He's spending three or four hours a day getting to his course by bike and anyway, he keeps threatening to disappear without warning."

"Oh. Same as always then?" responded Amy, rising to take dishes to the sink.

"Umm humm," said Lee. "Here let me help you with the dishes."

Picking up his coffee, Ben asked, "Where's this desk that wants restoring?"

Gus snagged the last piece of toast and led Ben towards the stairs. "It's solid oak, I think. Not a patina."

Lee glanced up, "Darn, is that clock right? I thought I had another hour. I'll have to leave you. with the dishes." Over her shoulder Lee asked, "Are you coming down to the rally later?"

"No. I'll finish the house today, if that's all right. Training tomorrow. I'm going to try an international class marathon next month."

"Great. See you soon."

Long after dark, Gus heard Lee coming in and went downstairs. Kicking her shoes off, she looked up and gave him a wan smile.

"Tough day?" he asked. "I saw on the news that quite a few people got arrested. Lot of rough-looking types, black T-shirts, scuffling with the police and screaming abuse at them. Of course that could just be what the media chose to show."

"Yeah, mostly Crows that got arrested. A few others but they were all catch and release. The Crows have their own lawyers, so not much for me to do. Just a long tiring day."

"So, what do I do to support you now? Leave you alone, run you a bath, get you some supper?"

"The best thing is, you asked. Can you bring the laptop into the kitchen?"

"If you don't need it upstairs, we could just leave it on the kitchen table."

"Hmm. Good. If you don't mind I'll stream some news. Is there any of that wine left from yesterday?"

"I'll get you a glass. Would you like an omelette?"

"Brilliant. After the news, I'll soak in a hot tub so that by the time I come to bed I'll be almost human again."

The next morning, they slept late. On his way to the kitchen, Gus collected the Sunday newspapers from the front porch. He put on coffee and settled down to read. A little later, Lee came down and joined him.

"We should take Sundays off whenever we can."

"Yeah. Just us time." He smiled in reply. "What would you like to do today?"

"When you made room in the garage to park your bike and trailer did you see my bicycle?"

"You mean that titanium, 48-gear, three-thousand-dollar abomination?"

"It is not! Anyway, I got it second-hand."

"Uh huh, well I put it on a wall hook beside mine. Would you like to cycle down to the sea? I feel like getting some salt air in my lungs."

"Great. I know a wonderful seafood place." Looking at him Lee asked, "Say, I've been wondering. What you'll do about the ride to your school in the winter?"

"I'll start being away for a few days at a time soon."

"You should put a calendar on the wall and mark when you'll be away," she said nodding towards a pegboard.

"We have a great selection at school, I'll bring one."

"I'll bet you do. How about one with big yellow machines on it?"

"If you insist. Our first practice job is to bulldoze basements. Remember those families I want to help resettle from an island to the mainland?" As Lee nodded, Gus continued, "Their new homes are going to be up in the hills, a ways out beyond the school. The job's what you lawyers call pro bono. We get to play with the big yellow machines, they get free basements."

Laughing she asked, "When's this going to be?"

"Week after next."

"That'll work. We have an exam for this seminar at the end of that week, so I'll be able to cram without neglecting you. Will you be home by the Friday?"

"Oh yeah. Probably early in the day."

"Great. The whole class will go out drinking. Significant others included."

"Oh. Am I significant or other?" he asked as he put the last of the cutlery into the dishwasher. Rolling her eyes, she asked, "How did you guys make out with the desk?"

"Pretty good. It's oak. We measured it, took pictures and Ben removed some sample pieces. It'll take him a while to find matching wood to use for repairs." He paused then inquired, "He asked about Amy. You know, is she attached?"

"Really? That's all right then 'cause she asked about him."

Soon enough they were peddling down the laneway in the beautiful end of summer sun.

Chapter Seven

"Hey Gus, can you help me please?"

"Sure." Gus trotted over to where Joe was working on the side of a big rig trailer. "What are you doing?"

"I replace the cog wheel for, uhh, tight, uh make tight..."

"Tightening," supplied Gus.

"Yes, tightening the straps, hold the load."

"Hey, I asked the maintenance shop to replace one on the rig I'm using. They told me the parts are so old they can't get them anymore. Where'd you get the cog wheel?"

"I make. Hold this strap, please."

"You made it. Cool. Were you a machinist back home?"

"Engineer. OK, pull the strap tight. Good, that's fixed. In my country everything is old. If we want to fix, we make." Joe shrugged, smiling.

"If you're an engineer why are you learning to drive a truck?"

"Already know how to drive a truck, just get paper."

"Yeah, but why not work as an engineer?"

"Drive truck is work I can get."

The course supervisor came up and inspected the replacement cog.

"Looks good, keep the old one just in case."

"Yes sir," Joe replied, bobbing his head nervously.

"All right if I head out for the weekend?" Gus asked the course supervisor. "Those folks are going to give me a lift."

"Sure. See you Monday."

Gus nodded to Joe and headed down the hill to a dilapidated truck. He climbed into the back; smiling and high fiving, he settled his back against the cab and the old pickup rattled off.

Half an hour later, the truck pulled into a side road and Gus hopped down. Waving his thanks, Gus walked off down the road. It took him almost an hour to reach the next sideroad and double back across the highway. Tramping along another gravel road, he felt rather than heard his tactical voice telling him to check for traffic before turning off into an overgrown pathway.

A few hundred yards farther down the track, he found himself standing in the shadow of a tree watching to see if anyone was following him. *Almost dark, pretty sure we have not been followed, need to pick up the pace.* Gus jogged along the path, crossed a small creek and pulled up at the edge of a clearing. *Good to check, could be hunters using this shack.* After watching and listening for few minutes Gus cautiously went into a tumbledown loggers' cabin and took some supplies from under an old tarp.

Outside he made a small fire and set a billycan of water to boil. With a hot mug of tea and a handful of granola, he settled down to enjoy the array of colours in the fading light. As it grew dark, he went inside, rolled himself into a sleeping bag and was soon asleep.

In the morning, he made can-bottom coffee, took another handful of granola and watched the dawn light seep back into the sky. As soon as he could see, he brought some equipment out of the shack. Using cement from his supplies with sand and water from the creek, he mixed concrete and poured a two-inch-thick slab in the bottom of an old duffle bag.

That done, he brought out a contraption made of black plastic pipe. *Do you really think this thing will shoot goop bombs a hundred yards or more?* Gus sat with another cup of coffee analyzing the pros and cons of his machine. 'Only way to find out is to shoot it.' Standing, he shook the kinks out of his legs, picked up the contraption and another duffle bag full of equipment and hiked off down the stream.

Upon reaching a long meadow, he obeyed his tactical sense by spending a while hidden in brush, waiting to see if anyone else was about. Satisfied he was alone, he pulled a can of compressed air, a pressure gauge, balloons to make water bombs, a funnel, rags and assorted tools out of his bag. He charged the plastic pipe contraption.

Not as easy as filling a car tire. Kneeling, he aimed down the meadow and fired; whoosh, the air pressure pushed the water-filled balloon out of the pipe so that it flew over the grass and exploded nearly a hundred yards away.

Satisfied, he tried again, but the second shot blew up in the barrel, spraying coloured water all over the place. For the next hour, he worked to fit balloons inside cartons, and put wadding around the water bombs, but he only succeeded in soaking himself and the surrounding bushes. Giving up for the day, he put everything back into the duffle bag and headed back to the shack. *Lessons learned. Need a better bomb but it must be soft, absolutely cannot hurt people.*

Back at the shack, he made himself another can of coffee. Happy to see that the concrete had set in the bottom of the duffle bag, he gathered up all his gear and cached it under the tarp. He made sure the fire was out by dumping the last of his coffee onto it, then set off along the path out of his camp.

Curbing his impatience, he carefully checked to make sure he was not seen, as he went back onto the road. A few hours later he reached the heavy machinery school. As expected, no one was around to see him unlock his bike and set off for home.

Coming in through the back door, he missed a phone call. Listening to the message, he heard Lee's voice telling him, "Meet us at 'The Dive.' Don't bother calling. All our cell phones are being turned off as I speak." Amused, he went up the stairs two at a time. In the shower, he took care to scrub himself and made sure no telltale traces of his morning's work remained.

He caught a bus downtown and within an hour was stepping into a cacophony of sound. Lee waved to him from a large table at the back of the room. A couple of people shuffled their positions and he was able to fit a chair in next to her. Almost immediately, a server arrived to look at him inquiringly.

"Got any Red Brick Special on tap?"

KILLING OUR GRANDCHILDREN

"Yes sir."

"I'll have a pint."

Collecting glasses and orders, the server disappeared into the throng, returning almost immediately with a drink-laden tray. Seeing his expression, a slim faced fellow told him, "Wi-Fi from server to bartender. All the server has to do is pick up the tray. I'm Rob by the way." He stretched across in front of Lee to shake hands.

Turning to his other side, Gus saw a woman with a pixie cut, who introduced herself as Julia. She then gestured to the man next to her saying, "This is Gerry." Gus and Gerry repeated the stretch and shake routine. Gus offered his hand to Julia who blinked then briefly shook it.

"You're another of the change now or kill everybody brigade, I suppose," said Gerry watching the server set down the pints of beer.

"Don't mind him. He's the class smart aleck," Lee said. Regarding Gerry, she went on, "I still think you're wrong. Enforcement is as important as the law."

"No. Strong laws will prevent pollution."

"Like our southern neighbour, best anti-pollution laws on the continent," Gus put in. "Problem is, nobody obeys them."

"Three points for the new boy," said Rob.

Gerry came back with, "The laws are to keep liberals off their back. They know climate change is a hoax."

Lee responded, "Not true. The current data on atmosphere shows a steady increase in temperature."

"We don't know that. I don't believe all this core sample mumbo jumbo."

"Darling, wouldn't it be a good idea to slow down the pollution so we will have time to find solutions?" asked Julia, who was clearly experienced at defusing situations.

Gus, trying to create a distraction, looked around and asked, "Do they serve food here? I haven't eaten since breakfast."

"Finger foods. Vegetable plates, stuff like that."

"Nachos?" Gus asked hopefully.

"What, not a vegan?" asked Gerry.

"He likes his steak practically raw," Lee said, forcing a smile and waving at a server.

"I could use something to eat as well," said Rob from the other side of Lee.

Thankful for a reason to turn away, Gus asked, "Are you the fellow who sails a Y Fourteen?"

Rob was soon describing the finer points of ocean sailing with dinghies. When the food arrived, Gus dug in gratefully. Scraping up the last of the cheese, he paused to look at the bowl carefully.

"It's a fibre shell with a bio-polyethylene lining," said Julia.

"Hmm. Never seen that kind of thing used with wet contents before."

In response to his interest, Julia explained, "Cups and semi-dry have been around for some time. The newer materials will last for about an hour with this kind of food. Still compostable, which is the point."

"You have impressive expertise," said Gus.

"I've an undergrad degree in biochemistry. While Gerry gets his law degree, I'm working with a company that develops biodegradable containers."

"Ha. Can't serve beer in the stuff," said Gerry as the server set down another pint of Red Brick in front of Gus.

"I didn't order that."

"I did. Gotta catch up boy," a grinning Gerry informed him.

Turning back to Julia, Gus asked, "Is any progress being made with hemp plastic?"

"Can't put beer in plastic. Won't taste right," slurred Gerry.

Diplomatically Gus said, "Well, glass bottles are reusable so that works."

"I thought we got water in hemp plastic bottles this summer," Lee stated looking at Julia.

"Yes, hemp plastic can be used commercially for water. The enforcement agencies are demanding long term trials before hemp plastic can be used to bottle anything like Cola."

"Cola's pretty powerful stuff. It's used to wash blood out of ambulances," put in Rob, obviously trying to keep a more conversational tone to the exchanges.

"All this gloom and doom," said Gerry. "You'd think the world was going to end."

"The world's going to be fine," Lee blurted.

"What's all the fuss about then?"

"Isn't there usually a DJ here?" Rob made a blatant effort to steer the conversation away from controversy.

"Will we survive? That's the real question," murmured Julia. Startled by her own voice, she raised a hand to her lips.

"I think we still have some chance," Gus said, trying to cover her discomfort.

"Ha," barked Gerry. "Even he doesn't believe what he's preaching."

Someone at the other end of the table called out, "Hey Rob, we're going on to Danni's. They've got a new band."

"Lee, does your new fella dance..."

Gerry belligerently growled at Gus, "What do you believe?"

Getting up, Gus turned to Lee and said, "I'd like to..."

"Come on. Tell us the truth," demanded Gerry aggressively.

Exasperated, Gus sat down hard and striving to keep his voice calm stated, "I think we've got eight to ten years before climate patterns are so disrupted that as a civilisation we can no longer cope with the changes. After that some very small groups of very wealthy people may be able to survive in heavily defended self-sufficient enclaves."

"Nobody believes that."

"The oil companies believe it. Decades ago, their research demonstrated the current climate disintegration. They just kept on making profits off of oil."

"That's ri-ridiculous. That's a conspiracy theory."

"Yeah, well better than the plagues getting us." In an effort to contain himself, Gus got up asking, "Where is Danni's?"

"Hey. Siddown. You can't just leave it like that."

Trying to muster a smile Gus said, "I'm ruining the party. Let's go dancing."

"Wait. What plagues? There's no plagues."

"Ebola. SARS. Every few years, a previously unknown virus begins to spread. Sometimes from small, isolated groups of people; other times the origins are less clear. Sooner or later, one will get loose. We won't be able to prevent the spread fast enough to develop a cure. Now, I really am going dancing."

Taking Lee's arm Gus followed Rob and most of the others.

Outside, Lee said, "Danni's is just up here. We can walk."

After a minute Gus said, "Sorry. I almost never go off like that."

"Have those been your beliefs all the time we've been together?"

"Pretty much."

"Do you think my father's part of that, uh, cabal?"

"Stay or go. My guess is the conglomerates whose wealth derives from oil are in the 'stay' group and are trying to find a way to survive on earth. The 'go' group are trying to leave using privately funded space programs. The speed of climate change is outstripping them. Getting large numbers of people into space is not happening anytime soon."

"Yes. But my father?"

"I really don't know, honey."

Lee looked at him apprehensively, then turned toward a raucous club with a huge dance floor. "This is Danni's."

"Oh, yeah. This is what I need." Gus went straight to the nearest bar. Laying down a fifty-dollar bill, shouting to be heard over the band he asked, "You got a dark bitter on tap?"

"Yes, we do," said the barkeeper, eyeing the bill.

"Whisky and a pint." Laying down a second fifty he said, "Keep 'em coming and let me know when the money runs out."

Next morning, pulling back the bedroom curtains, Lee chirped, "Rise and shine, sleepy head."

"Argh. Turn off the lights."

"That's beautiful sunshine," she said in a mischievously cheerful voice. "Come on, let's see some hustle. We promised to meet Rob at the Yacht Club before ten."

"Ohhh," groaning Gus staggered into the bathroom and stuck his head under the cold-water tap. Then, he began drinking glass after glass of cold water.

"Good. Good. Hydration is just what you need."

"What I need is coffee."

"No, no. That will just make you more dehydrated." In an implacably sensible voice Lee went on, "I'll make you a nice mug of herbal tea."

Gus began to complain before realizing she had left; he turned his attention to getting tepid water to run in the shower. Some time later, shaking himself like a dog, he lurched out into the bedroom and found Lee had laid out some clothes for him. Gradually coming to his senses, he thumped down the stairs and put on a pair of trainers.

She appeared from the kitchen with travel mugs in hand.

"Let's go."

Squinting, he said, "Wait, sunglasses."

As their bus rumbled through the port toward the ocean, he slowly came to life. When they began to smell sea salt in the air, he actually perked up. Arriving at the Yacht Club, they discovered Julia waiting at the gate.

"Rob's coming to sign us in."

Gus looked around cautiously, wondering how he was going to manage to keep a civil tongue. Julia giggled. "It's all right. Gerry's at home sleeping it off. I knew he would be, that's why I agreed to come."

Rob turned up and took care of the formalities with a decidedly jaunty air.

"Am I the only one with a hangover?"

"Seems so, old boy. Although considering the amount you took in, I'm surprised you're even standing," replied Rob.

"Old boy?"

"Did a year at Oxford. Picked up a few bon mots."

"Let me guess. A Rhodes Scholar and an Olympic sailor."

"Actually, I was only an alternate."

"What about you Julia? Skippered an around-the-world cruise, I expect."

Laughing Julia replied, "Only my third time sailing. Rob's been teaching me."

"A very apt pupil, I will say."

"Right." Turning to Lee, Gus said, "You two proto-Olympians can go three times around the buoys and come in. If Julia and I can get around the first buoy and back to dock before you, we win. And you're buying." He paused then added, "Food, no booze."

He and Julia had a good time, scudding about swapping the skipper and crew positions every now and then. Like everyone else at the club, they watched in awe as Rob and Lee made their craft skim over the water, swooping around buoys in the dazzling sunlight.

Once the dinghies were moored, the four of them went up to the clubhouse to enjoy a late lunch. Gus ordered tonic water.

"Poor baby still has a headache." Lee's impish smile reappeared.

"Just obeying your orders to hydrate." In an entirely obvious attempt to change the topic, he looked at Julia and asked, "What's the problem with making hemp plastic bottles viable for soft drinks or any liquid?"

"Nothing really. The regulatory agencies want yearlong shelf tests to see if any of the bottles leak. After that, they'll think of some other way to stall us."

"Should be like the aeronautics industry," put in Rob. "Company employees inspect their own products."

"Sorry. I didn't mean to start us off on a controversial topic."

"That's all right, old man. Everyone here is capable of civilized debate."

Taking the cue, Julia continued, "We're having better luck with fibre containers."

"Like the bowls we saw last night."

"Yes. We're well on our way to creating plant fibre cans."

"Like tin cans? For soup or vegetables?" Lee asked.

"Exactly. It was fairly easy to develop a method of making a strong tube. The problem was pretty much solved by extruding layers of fibres at right angles. Sort of like a paper plywood."

Gus leaned a little so the server could place a fresh tonic water in front of him. "Excellent salad, Rob."

"Glad you're enjoying it. New chef came in recently. Greatly improved the whole, umm, organic items side of the menu. Uses the hundred-mile approach, as much as he can."

"Some people still insist on swordfish steaks," added Julia, with a bleak expression.

In an effort to draw Julia away from her sad thoughts, Gus asked, "How do you make the tops and bottoms on these paper cans? I mean with tin cans you just weld them on."

"A lot of cans are punched now. We think we can match that by extruding into forms, which will make the base one piece, together with the sides. The next challenge is to attach lids. At the moment, we are experimenting with glues. Not very promising so far."

"I say, if you get it solved before I sail around the world, you can give me some for a 'real life' trial. What?"

"Daa-ling," Lee said, "you are rather laying on the Britishisms."

"Let me enjoy it. I've only been back a month. It'll wear off in no time."

"When is this round-the-world trip happening?" Gus asked.

"Probably leave the summer after next. I expect I'll need a rest by then."

"Rob's four years older than me," put in Lee. "At the rate he's going, I'll be called to the bar before him."

"Well, you know what they say about law school."

Playing up to him Julia assumed an expression of awe and asked, "No, what?"

"First year they scare you to death, second year they work you to death. So, I expect a round-the-world sailing trip will give me just the rest I need, after second year."

"What about third year?" Lee asked.

"Bore you to death. Be able to rest up from all that sailing by sleeping through the whole year. Probably won't miss a thing. Speaking of sleeping through things, do you still have season tickets for the symphony?"

"And opera. And classical theatre. Father insists I should become cultured, while living in the most metropolitan port on the western seaboard."

Julia's eyes sparkled. With a slight tilt of his head, Rob fractionally raised his eyebrows.

Catching his hint, Lee continued, "I'm always looking for people to give them to."

"I'm sure Julia would be glad to help you out," said Rob. "My recent sojourn in a truly civilized country has given me a taste for the finer things in life. Should you need an escort Julia, I would be glad to oblige."

"La Boehme is at the opera house next month."

"I don't know the date off hand, but I'll give the tickets to Rob. You two can sort it out."

"Oh, how very kind."

"However," Lee said in a mock serious tone, "you shall have to give me a thumbnail review so that I can convincingly pretend to have seen it. Or do you hear opera?"

Shaking his head Rob replied, "See opera. Hear opera. I don't know. Anyway, I can do that."

"Humph. I would much prefer that Julia called me. I've known you since grade school. I don't believe you are any more interested in opera than I am."

Rob looked as if he had been caught out. Julia giggled. In this manner, the four passed a pleasant afternoon, parting on good terms.

Chapter Eight

Later in the week, Gus came in wringing the fingers of his left hand.

"What's happened?"

"Twisted my fingers on a stiff control lever."

"There are frozen peas in the fridge."

"What? Artificially coloured, full of who knows what chemicals."

"I only use them for cold compresses," Lee explained defensively. "I used to keep dried chickpeas."

"What was wrong with them?"

"Every time I used chickpeas more than once, they'd turn into gooey mess, so I'd have to throw them out and I was always forgetting to soak a batch to put in the freezer."

Getting a bag of peas from the freezer Gus observed, "You're home early."

"I am. I even cooked."

"Hmmm," he looked at her skeptically.

"Don't worry. Even I can't mess up salad and cold cuts. Beer or wine?"

"Ah. Wine's good." Shifting his attention to her, he asked again, "How come you're home early?"

"Don't get used to it. We're about done with orientation."

"Wait up, didn't you already do orientation?" he asked.

"That was for the seminar, now it's for this year's degree courses. The grind will start again very soon. Then it's long nights in the library."

"And I thought undergraduate life was all beer and frivolity."

"Not if you want to graduate summa cum laude."

"Yeah. Well, like I warned you, I'll start being away quite a bit now. Perhaps we can coordinate so as to have some time together."

Lee asked, "What about Thanksgiving? I really want you to meet Aunt Agatha."

"Agatha as in the mystery writer?"

"Well, it's 'Agnes' really but she hates that name. She's always reading mystery novels though, so we dubbed her Agatha."

"Well, the thing is, if I take off Thanksgiving, then I have to work the Christmas week. I was rather looking forward to Christmas with you."

She looked at him with consternation. "I'll have to be with my family this Christmas. Every year Christmas or Thanksgiving is a command performance, everybody has to go to the ranch. This year it's Christmas."

"If your brother or anyone else is going to try and goad me into espousing my views, the whole thing could get rather fraught."

"Hmm. I'm afraid he would."

"Right then. Thanksgiving at Aunt Agatha's but I won't come to the ranch at Christmas."

"I'll mark that on the calendar."

"Did I mark on there that I will be away from tomorrow until the Sunday after next?"

Lee looked at the calendar. "So you did. OK. Well then, I won't start reading tonight," she said. "We could go see a movie."

"I'll have lots of time for movies over the next few weeks," he said running a hand lightly up her back. The impish glint appeared in her eyes.

Just before dark, the following Saturday, Gus humped a large pack of materials into the logging shack. After putting a pound of dried chickpeas to soak in a bucket full of water, he rolled himself into his sleeping bag.

The next morning, he sipped his coffee while tossing chickpeas at a rock. They made satisfying splats. Bringing his rucksack from the shack, he dumped it onto the ground and sorted the jumble of plastic pipes, cups and cans into piles of identical pieces. Through trial and error, he found a cup that fitted snugly into the pipe he was using as a barrel.

After lunch, with his original air cannon, charging bottle and some cups, he headed downstream to conduct firing trials in the clearing. A disastrous afternoon followed. His first attempt made a cup full of chickpeas disintegrate in the barrel. After washing it out, he tried again, only to have the muck sprayed all over him. Numerous other attempts were rarely more successful.

Discouraged, he went back to camp and took the cannon and a bucket upstream to a small pool. Once he had thoroughly cleaned the cannon, he washed his clothes. Next he used buckets of water to sluice off the gunk then put his wet clothes back on. *I told you to keep dry clothes here.* 'Know it all.'

Returning to the shack, Gus wrapped himself in the tarp and tried to sleep. Before dawn he woke cold and damp. Breaking camp in the dark, he went out to the side road with less caution than usual. As soon as he could, he began jogging to get more warmth into himself

He pulled out his watch and saw he had enough time to make the trucking stop about ten miles up the highway. Once there, he drank several cups of steaming coffee and devoured a stack of pancakes. A sympathetic trucker gave him a lift down the highway. By the time he got into the locker room at the heavy machinery school, it was still early. Gus threw his clothes into the company washing machine, wrapped a towel around himself and went into the lunchroom to put on a fresh pot of coffee. Coming out of the lunchroom, he bumped into Joe.

Looking at Gus's towel, Joe asked with a grin, "Say, you got a girl in there?"

Making a wry face, Gus answered, "Doing laundry. Coffee's hot."

Throwing his clothes into the dryer, he warmed himself up some more with a blisteringly hot shower. Clean and dressed, he clumped back into the lunchroom.

"Phew. What is that crud on your boots?" asked Joe looking up from his newspaper.

"Ugh. Don't know." Gus searched for a convincing lie. "Got off the bike to fix a loose chain. Must have picked up some filth."

Gus went outside to use the high-pressure hose to wash the chickpea goo off his boots. Joe followed him asking, "You still riding your bike?"

"Yeah. Not for much longer, if this weather keeps up."

Returning to the lunchroom, they began a game of gin rummy. Joe got up and rummaged through the cupboards. Eventually he returned to the table with a food container.

Gus teased, "Doesn't your girlfriend feed you?"

"We were in the city. Dvora had to leave early to get to her job so she dropped me off. Coulda had breakfast but..." Joe shrugged, "I can eat anytime."

"What are those things anyway?" Gus asked, eying the canister.

"Khebz. It's a flatbread. Better than pita."

"Mind if I try one?"

"Help yourself."

Picking up the canister, Gus asked, "Why are they in this tube?"

"If you eat them right after they are cooked, they're chewy. The tube is supposed to keep them fresh."

"These are kinda crunchy. More like crackers."

"Yeah. Tube's got some kind of coating. It should keep them moist and fresh but the khebz dries out pretty quickly once you open those paper cans."

"Where do you get them?"

"Some of the truck stops have them. Lotta long haul drivers from the Middle East."

"Must be somewhere in the port you can get them."

"Oh yeah. Ever been to that big Middle Eastern supermarket?"

"Down by the central square?"

"Yea, that's the one. You can get anything there. Fresh hummus, oh man."

"Never really liked hummus, myself."

"Gotta get the right ingredients. Can't make hummus with dried chickpeas. Just doesn't taste the same. You..."

Joe's voice faded out as Gus examined the package. It seemed to be corrugated cardboard with some sort of plug for the base. The inside was coated with a glistening material that looked metallic.

"What? You're more interested in the container than the food?"

"Last weekend I met a girl who designs these things. Got me interested. Can I have this?"

"Sure. Just give me the last khebz."

Laughing, Gus shook out the flatbread and tossed the container into his daypack. While they were talking some of the other students had wandered in. The course supervisor yelled through the door, "OK. Load up."

"Wait, are we all here?" someone asked.

"You know the rules. Here on time or find your own way," said the course supervisor bruskly. "We need to get a half day in at the site."

Gus climbed into the back seat of the van. Shoving his daypack up against the window, he went to sleep. At a rest stop, Gus hunted through the aisles until he found a couple of containers of flatbread while the supervisor put gas in the van. As Gus got back into the van, he tossed one of the tubes to Joe.

Joe's eyes lit up. "All we need now is some hummus."

Digging into another pocket Gus offered a plastic dip container, "How about this?" "Eh, I bought these chickpeas too, are they what you would use to make hummus?" Gus asked, pulling out a can.

"Ugh. Not those. The olive oil soaks in which is OK, until you start to cook them, then they fall apart. Makes the hummus taste like sand."

Just the thing for air cannon ammunition, opined the voice in his head, as Gus dipped a very small amount of hummus onto his khebz. By the end of the week, he had accumulated several canisters, although his taste for hummus had not improved.

On Friday, the crew was let go early, so Gus got to the logging shack with lots of light left. He pulled a bicycle pump out of his pack and began pressurizing the air cannons and checked his new ammunition cylinders. Next, he stirred green dye into the chickpeas and left them to soak.

He rummaged in his pack to find a half-finished cylinder of the flatbread and a jar of jam. With a cup of tea, Gus enjoyed his favourite time of day, watching the magnificent colours of the sunset glide across the blazoning leaves of the birch, maples and oaks.

The next morning, he quickly packed the cannon, ammunition, bicycle pump and assorted tools into his concrete bottomed duffle bag and set off for the shooting meadow. There were deer grazing across the open space when he arrived at his firing point, so he stood very still, looking and listening for a long time to be sure there were no hunters around.

Fairly certain that nobody was about, he proceeded to ladle the bright green chickpeas into empty flatbread cannisters then load up his air cannons. The practice firing went smoothly and the new canister ammunition worked well. Through experimentation, he found an angle of fire that sent the containers sailing along the meadow to splatter green chickpeas over a wide area.

Satisfied with the morning's work, Gus packed up and began walking back. A faint sound of voices was carried to him by the wind. *Careful now, be slow and quiet.* Gus got close enough to see two men in hunters garb standing at the shack's door. "Whoever he is, he's a woodsman."

"How do you know? Maybe it's a woman."

"Don't be silly. Let's have some lunch and leave our blinds and chairs."

"OK, but I'll be angry if they're gone next week."

Taking folding camp chairs from their packs the two men settled down to strip the wrapping off their sandwiches. Pouring themselves coffee from a thermos, they each added a generous slug of whisky to their cups.

"We're not leaving any of the booze," said one. The other nodded.

Gus settled down on his haunches in the mottled shadow formed of low hanging branches and waited. After the hunters had left, he waited another hour before he cautiously advanced into the clearing.

Looking with disgust at the litter of wrappers and plastic containers, he left it untouched, as he stepped to the door of the logging hut. Grateful that his gear had not been disturbed, he fitted most of it into the large rucksack, tossing a trigger mechanism and other junk into a corner. He hoped it would look like trash left by some paintballers. He wanted to clean up the hunters' garbage, but he knew they would notice and think it odd.

Before leaving the bush, Gus stopped to consider his options. The early arrival of the hunters meant he could not return, as planned, to the logging hut in the future. Cycling into the port with the heavy pack would be difficult and might draw attention. The only place to hide his stuff, that he could think of, was in a locker at the truck stop. He did not like it. Very early Monday morning, he would have to retrieve his gear, and take it with him to the job site. He did not like that either.

The whole escapade meant he would not get much rest, but it was the only idea he had. Gritting his teeth, he set off for the truck stop. Once there, he left his pack in a locker and started back down the highway to the school, then rode his bicycle through the dark wet night to get to the port. Arriving home, he wheeled his bike into the garage and locked up. Noticing Lee's workroom light was still on, he frowned and entered the house quietly.

Gus listened intently for a minute but hearing nothing, he opted to clean up before going upstairs; in the basement he put all of his clothes into the washing machine, scrubbed off his boots, flushed the residue down the sink, cleaned out his daysack, then got into the rec room shower where he scoured his skin in an attempt to remove the food dye. *Rubber gauntlets next time.*

Finally, he stumbled upstairs and peeked into Lee's workroom. She was slumped over a thick book with a pool of light around her. Gently, he shook her shoulder but she did not wake. 'She's in worse shape than me,' he thought. Tenderly, he picked her up and carried her into the bedroom where the rumpled sheets were thrown across the bed. Laying her down, he tugged off her jeans, rolled her onto her side, and pulled the covers up over her then climbed in beside her. She snuggled herself around him and made a contented sound without ever waking. He smiled.

Chapter Nine

A splatter of rain woke them midmorning. Lee looked blearily out of the window and grumbled, "Rob wanted us to go for the last sail of the season."

Stretching Gus clambered out of bed. "I'll make some breakfast."

Soon after Lee came down the stairs, saying into her phone, "Well, I should study."

Gus emphatically shook his head and mouthed, "NO!"

"Mmm, Julia will be there?" She listened for a moment then replied, "All right we'll come and look at your new seagoing yacht."

Looking at Gus, she grouched, "There'll be lots of time to see his yacht when midterms are over. I'm only going because Julia will be there."

"What's up with her?"

"As is to be expected, that moron Gerry is making her life miserable."

"He's letting her hang out with Rob?"

"I guess Gerry is studying today, like I should be."

Snorting Gus asked, "Last night is your idea of studying? First exam is on Tuesday, right?"

"Mmm. History of Activism from Vietnam to the Modern Era. The professor is about as pretentious as his course title."

"Today you will get some fresh air, and, with a little luck, some sunshine. Relax, think about something besides exams." He toasted her with his coffee cup.

Looking at the lime green splotches on his hands she asked, "What happened to you?"

" Hm?" He followed her eyes. "The fall colours were making one of the fellows in the group homesick for Holi. I helped him make a multi-coloured cake."

"Uhh huh." She looked at him steadily for a second then put on a perky smile and asked, "Holi, Hindu festival of colours, right?"

"Very good. This is food dye. It'll wear off soon."

"We'd better get going." Tilting her chin towards the window, she added, "I don't want to take the bikes in that muck out there. Do you mind if we take the bus?"

"Fine by me," he answered with well-concealed relief.

Once the bus was under way, Gus asked, "So this 'Activism' course isn't what you expected?"

"I was hoping it would be tactics for radicalizing groups of people. Like getting college kids at a conference to do a snake dance. Supposedly snake dancing desensitizes people so that, at the next demonstration they attend, they are more likely to charge the police."

"It's not that?"

"No. It's a tedious trivia hunt. For instance, did you know that on June 2nd, 1962..." She regaled him with tales of utterly useless information in a droll imitation of her professor.

When they hopped off the bus, a stiff breeze brought salt air off the ocean and drove the clouds back, allowing a little sun to get through. Julia met them at the gate and signed them in then chattered about the new yacht as she led them along the quay. Rob emerged from below deck wiping his hands on a rag. "Hello there. You two look knackered."

"Still with the Englishisms, I see."

"Oh, absolutely old boy, I may keep them forever."

"You should see this nifty little galley. We cooked breakfast this morning." Julia stopped and blushed.

"I haven't disconnected the propane tank yet. Why don't you make these two some coffee? They look as if they could use it." Rob rattled on, "Say old boy, do you think you could apply those bulging muscles to the clamps on the sea cocks? I can't shift them."

Lee went with Julia to make coffee and Gus went to thrash around in cold, smelly water. Half an hour later Julia stuck her head through the hatch and called, "Tea's up. I mean—coffee's ready."

Once they each had a mug of coffee, Rob announced happily, "Gus shifted those clamps so the water can drain out. That's the last of the jobs. They'll be able to lift it out and wrap it in plastic tomorrow. I know. I know." He held up his hands defensively. "It's the only effective way to preserve the hull through the winter."

"Did the bilge water do that to your hands?" asked Julia.

Uncomfortable with repeating his lie, Gus limped through the story of Holi and the many-coloured cake.

"Holi is in the spring. Why did he want to celebrate it in the fall?"

"I don't know. Maybe he just wanted an excuse to bake a cake."

"Julia, could you bring the rental van..." Rob paused awkwardly.

"It's all right, honey." Julia turned to Lee and Gus and announced, "I've broken up with Gerry. We're moving the last of my stuff to Rob's place."

Gus's exclaimed, "Thank goodness. I'm always afraid I'll start another fight."

"Rob," cautioned Lee, "you're in law school. Remember to study."

"Study. Incredibly overrated. I refuse to be scared by a bunch of stuffy old law professors." Shaking her head, Lee helped Julia load the van while Rob washed and stowed the last of the dishes then disconnected the propane tank. All four of them made a trip to Gerry's apartment and collected Julia's stuff. After unloading the van, they went out for dinner together. Rob insisted on paying the bill and Julia offered to give them a lift home before returning the van.

"Except I'm driving," insisted Rob.

"Certainly not, it's my rental."

Lee and Gus endured Rob's running commentary on Julia's driving during the ride home. With promises to see one another soon, they climbed out of the van and watched as Julia drove away. Rob's less than kindly remarks could still be heard, as they turned toward the house.

"There's nothing wrong with her driving," said Gus. "Why is he going on like that?"

"Insecurity? Ingrained beliefs about the proper place of women? Assumptions of superiority common to the children of oligarchic families? All my cousins have quirks of one kind or another. Not me of course," she added with a self-deprecating smile.

As they entered the house, Gus asked with uncharacteristic hesitancy, "I was wondering, if you would mind, if I borrowed your car for a few days?"

"Of course not. I mean, of course you can borrow it."

"It's just that this week the school says the job is close enough for everybody to drive but it's too far to cycle."

"And the weather is getting too cold to be cycling four hours a day. I'm glad you asked. I've been trying to figure out how to make a tactful offer."

"All right. I'll go and check the charger is plugged in."

A little while later Gus gratefully set his alarm so that he could get up a couple of hours later than he had originally planned. Lee was already fast asleep, as he got into bed beside her. In the morning, she woke as he was getting up, gave him a happy smile and went back to sleep.

The electric car managed the hilly part of the highway well, so he arrived at the school's collection point a little ahead of time. In the parking lot, close to the charging plugs, where there were lots of spaces; Gus parked the little electric car He got his duffle bag from the locker and put it in the car's cargo space. Finally, he slung a custom-made fabric cover over the vehicle.

Inside, at the coffee counter, Gus got his travel mug filled and bought a couple of iced donuts. There were no smart remarks about his 'healthy' breakfast. He finished eating just as the school van arrived to take the course members to the new job site. Gus climbed in, went into his usual spot at the back, rolled into the corner and was asleep before they were out of the parking lot.

This time, he only got a brief nap before the van bumped up a hill into the work site. The course supervisor twisted in his seat and announced, "All right lads. Get this bulldozer job done right and we'll be able to go home on Thursday."

To nobody's surprise, the job was finished Thursday morning and the van arrived to ferry them back to the drop off point. Gus got the electric car started and moved it a couple of spaces to the charging point. After making sure that the charger was working properly, he went into the diner. Joe and a couple of the others were in a booth playing three-handed euchre.

Sitting down, he said to Joe, "Surprised you haven't left yet."

"Even as you speak, my Dvora arrives," Joe exclaimed cheerfully as he pushed out into the aisle. "Happy Thanksgiving guys."

Gus picked up Joe's cards and began to play them. When the waitress arrived, he ordered a hot beef sandwich with onion rings. The three of them finished the game and chatted for a while as the others waited for friends to pick them up. By the time Gus had finished his meal, all the guys from the school were gone.

As soon as the car was fully charged, Gus drove off. At his destination, he turned off the highway into a small city and found a long-term parking garage with charging points. Opening the car's cargo area, he lifted out his daysack and the concrete bottomed duffle bag with his air cannons in it. Next he spread the fabric cover over the car to hide its make and licence plate. *Not that somebody couldn't look under the cover, but why would they?* Gus grimaced as his tactical voice began rattling on.

Walking toward the city centre, he spent as much time as he could reconnoitring side streets and alleys. Early in the evening, he checked into a cheap hotel; he did not want to be remembered as the guy who checked in late at night, paid cash but had no companion.

Gus woke at his customary five AM. He rolled out of bed and pulled on a pair of disposable latex gloves and began by charging his air cannons. After that he practiced packing and unpacking the bag with cannons and ammunition, then stood the duffle by the door.

Next, he got into the shower where he carefully scrubbed off his whole body. He had seen this in a movie, supposedly the scrubbing would remove any loose hair or skin that could leave DNA traces. *Always the optimist.* 'Can't hurt.' Before leaving the room, he took a careful look around to be sure he had not left anything that would identify him.

With the surprisingly light duffle on his shoulder, he stepped out into the dim morning light. Walking across a bridge, he paused at the midway observation point to look over the railing. Gus was glad to see a swift current in the dark water. He continued a few hundred yards along a main thoroughfare toward the park, which held his target. As expected, he found a super sized gas station with a coffee shop. The place was already busy with early commuters. Going in at the side entrance, he was relieved to find large washrooms that had multiple stalls.

The park that held his target was bordered by homes for affluent, but not rich, people. Exactly the kind of voters a politician would want to influence by sponsoring an 'environmental' playscape. Gus did a quick scout of the park and chose an ornate green bench as his firing point. He did not want to be noticed and remembered, so he moved off down a side street to a small memorial. Leaning against a tree, he did his best to wait patiently.

Finally, it was time to get into position. He went past his firing point, gratified to see a fairly substantial crowd listening to their Mayor start the proceedings with a typically political speech. "I am pleased, at the opening of this 'Memorial Environmental Playscape' to welcome our corporate sponsors..."

Gus went into the park's public washrooms and entered the first empty stall, opened his duffle bag and pulled out a set of para-military camos. Struggling in the confines of the stall, he got into them and swapped his blue ball cap for a camo hat. With the duffle bag on his shoulder again, he exited the stall and strode out of the small building.

Tugging his hat to make sure it was obscuring his face from the lenses of any media cameras, he marched up to his firing point. Swiftly he pulled the air cannons out of the duffle bag and dropped cannisters of chickpeas down each of the barrels.

Ready to fire, he realized that the dignitaries were moving forward in preparation for cutting the ribbon. *Perfect timing. Don't mess it up.* Flipping the trigger cover clear, he squeezed gently and felt a satisfying thump as the canister flew away. Taking up the second air cannon, he examined his target. Noting the splatter falling at the correct range but a little too far to the left, he shifted his aim for the next shot.

As soon as the cannon had been fired, Gus packed everything into the duffle bag. But he couldn't resist looking to see what his green chickpea bombs had done to the crowd. Spectators were shaking their umbrellas and picking at the colourful green splotches. *Stop gawking. Get going.* Gus set off for the coffee shop, careful to keep a slow steady pace.

He was able to slip in through the side door without attracting attention but there were people in the shop's washroom. In the furthest stall, he hastily took off his outer camouflage pattern clothing. Haphazardly, he stuffed boots, camo pants and coat into the duffle. Gus pulled on a pair of trainers then shrugged into a windbreaker. He checked he was leaving nothing behind, then opened the stall door and came face to face with his image in the mirror. The cubicle door slammed closed as he ducked back, swept the camo hat off his head and shoved it into the duffle bag. Hoping nobody had noticed, he moved out of the washrooms, through the side door of the coffee shop and off towards the bridge.

At the viewing point in the middle of the bridge, he paused and leant against the railing. Gus got a prickly feeling. *Something's wrong.* 'Just nerves'. He overrode his tac voice and casually slid the concrete bottomed duffle bag over the railing and let it drop. He heard an indistinct splash as he walked away.

Risking a quick glance over the railing, he came to an abrupt halt. He stared at the duffle bag floating downstream. As he tried desperately to think of some way to make it sink, the bag tipped over, took in water and was swallowed by the fast-moving current. *Get going, later you can think about better ways to get rid of the evidence.*

Pulling himself together, Gus set off for the car park by a long, roundabout route, hoping that nobody had noticed him or would try to follow him. Eventually he arrived at the car. Relieved to see the timer had worked and the car had a full charge, he drove off down the highway listening to local radio stations. He was disappointed to hear the only mention of his action in a 'human interest' story about a playscape opening being briefly interrupted by a 'shower.' No mention of lime green chickpeas.

Arriving home fairly early, he plugged in the car. *You know, this car links you directly to your girlfriend.* 'Thanks for cheering me up.'

Entering through the back door, Gus caught the burnt smell that meant Lee had been cooking. In the kitchen, with a large glass of wine in one hand, she was scrolling through video posts about baking.

Glumly, Lee looked at him. "I'm supposed to make pumpkin pie for Thanksgiving dinner."

"The store was all out? You couldn't buy one?" he asked teasingly.

"Very funny. I always try to bring the ice cream. Nobody expects me to bake, but Uncle Albert is arriving late so he claimed ice cream, by necessity."

"Albert and Agatha? Are you kidding?"

"No. No. He's not Agatha's husband; he's another Uncle. What am I going to do?"

"We could scrape the black off the crust then..." Gus did not finish as a wadded dish towel flew toward him and Lee was clearly looking for something more substantial to throw.

"Oh, all right. As it happens, I make an excellent pumpkin pie. We'll have to use canned filling though, there isn't enough time to make it from scratch."

"I might have known." Lee smiled and poured him a glass of wine

Chapter Ten

The next morning found Gus sitting on a bench in front of the local grocery store with a newspaper, coffee and donuts.

"Hello. You're here early."

The bright voice brought him out of his reverie. "Hello, Amy. I didn't know this store was closed until eight o'clock. Fortunately, the donut shop opens earlier."

"Yes," replied Amy with a flicker of a smile. After a moment she added, "I hope you haven't run out of anything."

"We sure have. Oh. Not your fault. We're to bring pumpkin pie tomorrow for Aunt Agatha's extravaganza. I left the pie plates soaking and came to get the supplies for a second try."

"What happened?" Light dawned in Amy's eyes. "Yes, well they have excellent baking supplies here."

With Amy's help, Gus got everything he needed and she did the weekly shopping. Together they set off for the house, yakking about nothing in particular. Ben pulled up in his dilapidated truck just as they arrived home.

"Well met," said Ben.

"Let me drop this stuff in the kitchen, then I'll come and help you unload," Gus told Ben.

"Shall I start some breakfast?" asked Amy.

"Sure. Those donuts weren't very filling. Ben, you eaten?"

"Can always eat more. Especially if the company is convivial," replied Ben with a grin.

Lee appeared at the doorway saying to Gus, "Here, give me those. I've already made coffee if you want some."

"Ah. The joy of my heart," he said, giving her the baking supplies and a quick kiss.

"Me or the coffee?"

"You, of course." Gus grinned over his shoulder as he went back to help Ben with toolboxes and oak panels.

"Good answer."

Happily, the four went about their tasks. Gus helped Ben get set up to work on the desk. Lee scrubbed out the pie plates while Amy cooked. After breakfast, Ben went back to work on the desk. Amy cleaned the house and did laundry. Gus baked pumpkin pies. Lee wandered about with a textbook in hand and helped whenever asked.

By late afternoon, Lee was putting away the last of the laundry when Gus poked his head in the bedroom door, "Where's Amy?"

"Taking a shower."

"Think they'd like to join us at the movies?"

"I'll ask her. Supper out though, we've done enough dishes for one day."

"I'll ask Ben."

"My treat," she called to his retreating back.

So it was, a few hours later, they ended up sitting in a quiet corner of the local bistro finishing their meal.

"I think that movie establishes a new genre," Gus said genially.

"How so?" Lee asked with the sound of a donnish query in her voice.

"Well, you know, female superhero, spaceship captain," he said striving for an innocuous expression.

"Ah. And what should this new genre be called?" she asked as though leading a not very bright undergraduate through an intellectual process.

"Uh. I made rather good progress with the desk today," interjected Ben, apparently concerned that a spat of some kind was developing.

Amy assured him, "Don't worry Ben. They always go on like this,.

"Oh. I need to be going. Long drive tomorrow. Do you need a lift, Amy?"

"Umm, I live down towards the island. It's out of the way for most people."

"No. Not at all." Turning to his hostess, he said, "Thanks Lee. If it's all right I'll be back next Saturday to work on the desk."

"Sure. You know where the spare key is. Just give us a heads up."

They watched the tall willowy woman and the short broad man walk towards the pub's exit.

"Odd couple," Gus commented.

"Seem to get along well though."

"You're matchmaking," he said as he skidded around the end of the table to sit opposite her.

"Why are you sitting over there?"

"So that it will be harder for you to hit me while I explain the parameters of the 'feminist superhero' genre."

A little later as they strolled towards home Lee murmured, "The female superhero has been around for a very long time you know."

"How so?"

"Terracotta warriors or Viking shield maidens to name a couple that are no longer bywords of history."

"Mulan, Boudicca, Malalai of Maiwand, I was only teasing. You knew that."

Lee hugged his arm in silent acknowledgement. They continued contentedly home.

The next day Gus followed Lee through the door of Aunt Agatha's into a tumult of people with a pie in each hand. A big cheerful bustling woman met them and led them into a side room. "Put the pies down here."

As they set four pies on a counter Gus said, "I'm not sure we brought enough."

"Of course you did." Agatha opened her arms to hug him, and then checked herself. "Is it all right if I give you a hug?"

"Uh. Sure."

Engulfing him, she leaned her head close to his ear and whispered, "Don't worry. I know how well she bakes so I arranged some backup." Her niece was the next to receive a hug as Agatha commented loudly, "These pies look absolutely scrumptious."

Laughing, Lee admonished Agatha from the confines of the bear hug, "You know perfectly well I didn't bake them."

Ignoring Lee's confession, Agatha led them towards the living room announcing, "Albert is on his way from the airport, we'll eat in about an hour."

Taking Gus's arm, Agatha became a doting aunt. He was introduced to a plethora of relatives as 'beau,' 'boyfriend,' 'partner,' and, to his amusement, as 'the baker.' Eventually, with no idea where his 'partner' had disappeared to and no hope of keeping all the relatives straight, he settled into a quiet corner. Within moments, an older man with the unmistakable demeanor acquired from life-long service in the military appeared beside him and pushed a beer into his hand. Gus sipped his beer while politely listening to a long discourse on the tactics that should be used in Afghanistan.

Uncle Albert arrived with the ice cream and Lee appeared at his elbow. Disengaging him from the armchair strategist, she settled him into a chair at the middle of the dining table and slipped in beside him. "Sorry about Uncle Harold," she muttered under the babble of many guests and excited children.

Glad that there would be one person he knew sitting beside him, Gus leaned over to inquire, "Are you the only progressive in your family?"

Lee's answer was pre-empted by Aunt Agatha pronouncing from the head of the table, "Come on now, Lee. You know the rules. You aren't allowed to sit by your beau. Besides, Uncle Albert hasn't met him yet."

With a look of apology, Lee rose from her seat and a large man with the air of contrived joviality common to all salesmen squeezed in beside Gus. "How ya doin', I'm Albert. Sell aeroplanes for your beau's daddy." Shaking the proffered hand, Gus caught a warning look from his 'beau' who was now seated opposite him.

Albert abruptly stopped talking as there was a general shushing and the room quieted down. Directing her gaze to Gus, Agatha said, "It is our tradition to have new friends give the blessing. If you would be so kind."

He stared at Lee, dismayed, then looked down at the table. "Well Lord, it's been quite some time since you heard from me. The last grace I gave probably went something like 'Rub a dub, dub, thanks for the grub.'" There was a stifled giggle from the children's table. "You'll pardon me if I take a few moments to contemplate what I might best say."

He gazed at the saltshaker in front of him for so long that a little restlessness was beginning, and then he raised his head and began to speak. "Lord, as you may remember I am not much given to public speaking and in this case 'someone,' who shall remain nameless, forgot to warn me that I would be called on." There was a quiet burble of suppressed amusement. He continued, "This is rather august company for the likes of me to be asking for a blessing. As I recall I have been introduced to a priest and at least two pastors since I arrived. One of the pastors was a woman so I give thanks that you have helped us improve ourselves, so that we accept women as fit to be thy servants. I ask, Lord, that soon you will help His Holiness to follow our example, so that his sisters in faith will be treated as equal to his brothers in Christ." The room had stilled. There were some furtive glances at the priest seated beside Agatha. "I thank you Lord for this sumptuous feast which we are about to enjoy." This more commonplace invocation caused the tension in the room to relax somewhat, until Gus went on, "I beseech you Lord that we will be able to stay the destructive ways of humankind and return this planet to the beautiful garden which you gave to us. I hope that in years to come, our children's children will be able to give thanks at an equally bountiful table."

The silence had returned and Gus could hear some fidgeting from the children's table. He stared at the table knowing he had forgotten something but unsure what to do.

The priest rescued him by intoning, "In Jesus Christ's name. Amen."

The whole room burst into a babble of relieved voices chorusing, "Amen."

Then, having adeptly recognized the mood in the room, the priest gave his blessing by raising his glass in toast and declaring, "Well said, young man."

Under the clatter of serving dishes, Uncle Albert muttered, "Supposed to be a blessing not a sermon."

A gray-haired lady seated on the other side of Gus patted his arm saying, "Thank you, young man."

He ate sparingly, eschewed the wine, drank copious amounts of water and held his tongue while Uncle Albert rambled on about the benefits of retaliatory tariffs. Lee watched Gus from the other side of the table and following his lead, she drank sparingly and listened without comment.

Dessert had been served. Pies extravagantly complimented. The children were off roaring around in the living room. Coffee was being sipped. People were unobtrusively attempting to determine the time, an activity complicated by general reliance on cell phones rather than wristwatches.

For no apparent reason, Uncle Albert launched into a tirade about the detrimental effects on trade caused by the carbon tax. This stirred a hitherto quiet young woman at the far end of the table to note that carbon dioxide emissions had dropped in areas where the taxation had been introduced. Albert maintained that the evidence was inconclusive and that the oil industry was doing everything it could to encourage environmental responsibility.

Apparently attempting to divert the conversation, a middle-aged man asked everyone, "Have you seen that enviro clip that went viral?"

There was a general shuffling as almost everyone took the opportunity to bring out a cell phone or tablet and check the time under cover of searching for the clip. "Just search 'environmental playscape' and you should find it."

Soon several different versions of the video could be seen and heard around the table. Surprisingly, the elderly lady beside Gus had brought out a phone with a rather large screen. "I need it to make the text large enough for me to read," she explained, as she adroitly found the clip.

Gus set his face to prevent any unwanted reactions from showing and watched a very short clip of a man smiling disdainfully as he turned his face up into a light rain. Some lime green streaks on his cheeks and forehead were washed away.

"That can't be all of it," exclaimed Gus's neighbour.

"No, it isn't. But it 's very clever," the woman was giving a running commentary as her fingers flashed across the base of her screen. "Try this search string."

She read off a series of words that Gus's elderly neighbour typed into her screen to bring up a different clip. This time the term 'environmental playscape' was evident as a group of suited men gathered at what appeared to be a ribbon-cutting ceremony, then small lime green balls spattered down. The dignitaries were shown scattering except for one man, apparently a corporate representative, who turned his face up into the rain.

"What 'playscape'?" huffed the elderly lady, looking up from her screen. "That's just a jungle gym."

"Yes," agreed the younger woman. "Effective new use of the old 'Oil Corporation Bike Stand' strategy." Gus looked at her inquiringly. "Find an environmentally neutral, or even positive, installation or project that some politicians are using to use to gain support. Say, an outdoor play area, in a park, close to a neighbourhood where a politician wants to get votes. The oil corporation offers to pay for the installation if the politicians will plug the corporation's support for the project's 'environmental benefits.' Eh voila, act locally to defeat so-called climate change alarmists."

Albert walked right into the opening she had given. "So what? Nobody cares about stuff like that. Except, maybe, a few middle-class parents."

"Exactly. Only someone tried to use this event to raise awareness of climate change by dumping lime green stuff onto the corporation's representatives."

"Hey. How do you know so much?" demanded Albert.

"My job. I track social media for Environmental Watch. This was a clever action: anonymous, non-toxic materials, got a little coverage on the enviro blogs. It's the way the corporate guy looked up into the rain that made it go viral."

"I don't understand," Gus's elderly neighbour commented.

"The full-length clip threatened to undermine the corp's 'we're responsible citizens' spin on the event. Their response was clever. They didn't deny or start huffing and puffing about it. That would have given the environmentalists something to talk about. Some corporate PR guy caught it early, took a very short clip and saturated the video services with it, burying the original clip, and creating a mocking meme for the right."

"Good job. You enviro guys have got the wrong end of the stick," stated Albert.

"Love to debate you on that but my sitter will be counting the minutes until I'm home," replied the young mother in her disarming manner. "Agatha, thank you for yet another sumptuous feast."

This triggered a general rising of young couples, gathering of children and accepting, under feigned protests, the huge containers of leftovers. Gus and Lee were able to slip away amongst this cheerful chaos.

Crunching through the leaves Gus looked thoughtfully down at the path, as they walked towards the car. Fearing she had contributed to his despondent frame of mind, Lee said contritely, "I'm very sorry I didn't warn you about the grace. Truly, it never entered my head."

"Never mind, it livened up the whole proceedings," came a lighthearted voice from behind them.

Turning they saw the Environmental Watch woman coming along behind them with a huge box of leftovers. Indicating the box she added, "Aunt Agatha is afraid I'll starve to death before I grow out of my annoyingly persistent 'rebellious phase.'"

Laughing Gus said, "You made some excellent points."

"As the saying goes, that and a million dollars will get me a soapbox."

When they came up alongside her car, Lee said, "We'd offer you a ride but as you can see, it's a two-seater."

"Car manufacturers do that on purpose. Making electric vehicles practical might improve sales."

Gus looked at Lee. "Why don't you give," turning slightly he asked, "sorry, I don't know your name...?"

"My cousin, Natalie," Lee supplied.

"Why don't you give Natalie a ride home, then come back and pick me up. I'll walk up Main."

"Oh. I couldn't impose like that."

"Really. I want to think about how the media coverage was spun and walking will help. Besides, climbing on and off buses with that box of goodies will take all the fun out of the evening."

"Sure. That'll work." Lee looked at him. "It'll take about half an hour before I pick you up."

"Good. Nice to meet you Natalie."

Later as they plugged in the car and locked up, Lee asked, "You're not mad at me?"

"No. Why would I be mad at you?"

"About the grace thing."

"Uh. Oh no. I always regret not having the easy manner, which would let me say something that fits in and doesn't upset anybody."

"Well, the whole environmental thing was Uncle Albert's fault."

"Yeah. What do you think got into him?"

"Probably wanted something juicy to report to my father."

"What do you mean?"

"I told you, my father keeps very close track of me."

"Jeez." Shaking his head Gus asked, "How well do you know Natalie?"

"We've never been close. Her part of the family are not exactly black sheep but they're not enthusiastic industrialists either. Why, do you like her?"

"Didn't she say she had a baby?"

"She's a single mother. Her girl must be five or six by now. Do I need to be worried?"

"About what?"

"You and her?"

Shaking his head, Gus said mockingly, "You're as suspicious as your father. Anyway, you'll have her hooked up with somebody before I can find out where she lives."

"You know where she works. Environmental Watch."

"Oih." Rolling his eyes, he determinedly changed the subject. "One more day then back to the grindstone. What do you want to do tomorrow?"

Chapter Eleven

'Tomorrow' turned out to be a beautiful autumn day. As they finished breakfast, Gus suggested, "Let's take the water taxi over to the island."

"I thought you said that almost everyone was up at the new site, building homes and barns."

"Yes, next year there will be nothing left. This will be the last Thanksgiving on the island."

"All right then."

A couple of hours later they were huddled together in the bow of a water taxi that dropped them off at the island beach. Buffeted by a wind that blew in across a thousand miles of ocean, the pair made their way to the wooden church tucked away under the meagre protection of a low hill.

Inside Gus admitted, "Places like this make me think perhaps there is a God." He showed Lee the carved pews and hand-crafted beams that had stood for nearly a hundred years.

"Will you be able to save it?"

"We'll try. Of the original five houses, there are three that we were able to disassemble and rebuild at the community's new inland location. We're pretty sure we can lift the other two intact, load them onto flatbed trucks to transport, use barges to carry the loaded trucks across the sound, then drive to the new location."

"I don't really understand."

"You've probably seen house components being moved that way."

"House components?"

"Yes. There are companies that prefabricate full-sized houses in two pieces. They truck them to a building site, put them on a foundation and bolt them together."

"Hmm I might have seen those on the highway with 'Long Wide Load' signs."

"Yeah, that's it. The island's houses were built decades ago and are a little narrower. We should be able to move them without too much difficulty."

Gus looked up at the roof beams. "With the church we'll take off the spire and take out the leaded windows, of course. He pursed his lips. "The church is beam and peg construction. No nails or screws. We must transport the whole building in one piece. It's hard to see how we'd be able to dismantle it. I hope we can move it successfully."

"It will be as God wills."

Turning to the sound of the voice, Gus extended his hand. "Hello Elder Luke. This is my friend Lee."

Letting go of Gus's hand, Elder Luke gently took Lee's hand in his. "Welcome, Sister."

"I brought Lee to see the island before we start churning up the ground with trucks and diggers."

"It would make Mother happy if you could join us for luncheon. It will be leftovers, I'm afraid."

"Thank you. Do we have time for a walk along the shore?"

"Of course, my boy. Of course. We'll see you later."

Curiously, Lee looked up at Gus, as they turned into the wind. Seeing the sorrowful expression in his eyes, she did not speak.

Even leftovers made another bountiful meal, after which they caught a ride across the sound with a work group going inland to continue building the new homes. At the boat landing, Gus and Lee waved goodbye. Approaching their car, Lee moved towards the passenger side but he held up the keys saying, "Please drive."

"Sure."

Gus settled into a pensive silence as Lee drove. He roused himself as they reached their neighbourhood and began to explain, "The biggest problem is the size of the church. Not the actual moving. We should be able to manage that. To do it though, we would need to get the highway closed down. Probably for ten or twelve hours."

"That would be political. And very difficult."

"Hmm. Some sort of 'Save the church' campaign to put enough pressure on the government."

"Natalie might be able to determine the feasibility of raising that kind of public support."

"Oh. Now you're throwing me at Natalie."

"That's practically the first smile I've seen all day. Seriously, Environmental Watch is well placed to develop that kind of thing."

Some of Gus's brittleness softened. Going into the house they agreed that after so many gargantuan meals, a glass of wine would suffice for supper.

As the autumn weeks passed by, their life settled into a routine. Lee studied almost all the time except when Gus pulled her away from her books on Sundays. Amy continued housekeeping and Ben often turned up to work on the desk. Then Gus and Ben began to spend Saturdays puttering about on other projects. Eventually, to no one's surprise, Amy and Ben began to arrive together.

Sometimes the three of them could drag Lee away from her books for a Saturday night out. On one of these occasions, Julia convinced them all to attend a production of 'The Pirates of Penzance.' After the show, the whole group was waiting in line to be seated in one of the port's most expensive restaurants. Rob was recounting an incident from their childhood in which Lee had burrowed under the tablecloth to discover what kind of wood the table was made of.

"I wanted to see if it was as shiny as Gramma's dining room table."

"Our server was intensely embarrassed."

"That glorious antique cherry wood in your house." Ben smiled, as he asked, "Was it?"

Indignantly Lee stated, "It was not. There was a two-inch felt mat on top of old barn boards painted blue."

As she spoke, the maître d' appeared beside them.

"Ah, Miguel, we were just talking about you."

"I'm terribly sorry, sir, miss. I was not informed that you would be dining with us this evening."

"That's all right Miguel," Lee assured him. "We did not make a reservation."

"Miss, neither you nor the young man's families ever need a reservation with us. Please follow me."

Gus was about to protest because they were jumped ahead of several other groups waiting for tables. He got one of Lee's narrow eyed looks and subsided with a shrug.

As they entered the restaurant Lee said, "Oh look, there's my cousin Natalie," tipping her head towards the lounge. "I'll just say hello."

Lee was off before anyone could respond. Sliding into the seat beside Natalie, she smiled warmly and asked, "What brings you here?"

"I was invited by a network executive but apparently I'm being stood up," replied Natalie with a touch of melancholy.

"Oh dear. How very unkind."

"Comes with the public relations territory. I wouldn't really mind except I've been nursing this drink for an hour." Natalie looked at it glumly and added, "It'll set me back a week's worth of groceries."

"Ah. Well, you're free for dinner so you must join our party." Taking Natalie's arm Lee steered her towards their table saying to the maître de, "Miguel, please make room for one more at our table."

"We'll add a place immediately, miss."

"Really I..." Natalie tried to protest.

Arriving at the table, she told Natalie, "Really you must join us. Rob and I are treating this group of the unwashed to a proper meal. Now, you remember my 'beau' from Thanksgiving."

"Nice to see you again Natalie. Please come and sit beside me so I can see which cutlery I'm supposed to use." Frowning slightly Gus added, "Err, you do know how to use all these fancy implements?"

KILLING OUR GRANDCHILDREN

Lee gave Natalie a slight push in his direction. There was some discrete shuffling as Miguel supervised the setting of an additional place. When everybody had settled in, Lee said, "Now Miguel, just put everything together on my family account."

Allowing the maître d' to seat her, she winked at Rob. "I do enjoy imitating my father sometimes."

"Natalie, I do hope you have fond memories of me." With mock contrition Rob added. "Most cousins seem to think the last time they saw me, I was trying to put their pigtails into an ink pot."

"Tut-tut, Rob, that's a reference to 'Anne of Green Gables,'" said Julia. "This is a Gilbert and Sullivan evening."

"So sayeth Julia, our cultural attaché, and my darling 'Yum Yum.' Next to her is Ben, an artisan who does magnificent work restoring antique furniture. Then his paramour, Amy, in training for yet another marathon and of course our cousin Lee, who needs no introduction."

"Rob, law school is wasted on you. You should become a public relations executive." Taking up the menu, Lee mischievously added, "We should start with the snails."

Gus groaned. "Haven't we had enough cultural indoctrination for today?"

Even Julia looked relieved when Lee said, "Oh all right. But let's be a little more adventuresome than steak and potatoes."

There followed several courses of a connoisseur's delights. Amy, it turned out, was something of a gourmand, talking knowledgeably about the preparation of the various dishes. Rob examined the wine list carefully, and tasted the wines before allowing them to be poured.

"He's always been a wino," explained Natalie. "When I was about twelve he tried to get me drunk so that he could kiss me."

"It was a rather expensive bottle of Rothschild Beaujolais, as I recall. My father was furious."

Eschewing the cheese and fruit, they settled for coffee with a selection of sweet meats.

"We're not going to be expected to drink port and smoke cigars, are we?" Gus asked, causing Ben to snort coffee into his cup.

Natalie laughed outright for the first time since joining them. Rob smiled at her saying, "That's better. It's all right Ben, I'll forgo the cigars tonight although they do have some excellent vintages of port."

"Do you come here often, Natalie?" asked Amy. "They serve an exquisite cuisine."

"They do. Far beyond my pocketbook, I'm afraid."

"Some weaselly media cad stood her up," Lee explained.

"Cadess," amended Natalie. "Is that a word?"

Without pause, Gus asked, "How does Environmental Watch select its projects?"

"A plethora of issues are brought to us. We'd like to work on them all but we just don't have the resources. First we look for a core of activists who are going to do the work."

Julia's brow wrinkled as she asked, "You mean, all an issue needs is supporters and you'll work on it?"

"Oh no. Certainly not. There are thousands of groups supporting all kinds of nonsense."

"What are your criteria, besides the volunteers?" Gus asked.

"A few years ago, we had a huge internal debate over what kind of issues to support. The deliberations took several months. Ultimately it became clear we needed to settle on one issue in order to have any impact."

"Climate change," stated Ben.

Startled Natalie looked at him. "Yes."

"He doesn't talk much but when he does it's worth listening," said Amy with evident pride. "Why not plastic? It's killing the ocean ecology," asked Lee.

"Or toxic waste?" asked Rob. "It's killing people."

"Trying to fix everything would fritter away your resources. Meanwhile the globe would continue to warm and kill all of us," suggested Julia.

"Exactly. That's what makes the issue of climate change the most consequential."

"Unless some half-witted politician starts a nuclear war," suggested Rob.

The conversation shifted to a dissection of upcoming elections. They lamented the years of effort and investment it took to develop political influence and how easily that influence could be undercut by corruption.

"Gilbert and Sullivan said it all," opined Rob. "The subtleties of the legal mind are equal to the emergency."

"Isn't that from 'Iolanthe'?" asked Lee, yawning. "Excuse me. Unlike my compatriot, I study a lot and sleep little."

"You'd be surprised," remarked Julia. "He's always reading something, night or day."

"I'll just see to signing the account," said Lee, gently lifting an eyebrow.

"I'll take care of Miguel," put in Rob. Gus watched in amazement as Rob, keeping his wallet out of sight of the others, pulled out and folded several fifty-dollar bills. Catching his expression, Rob explained, "Expected of my class, old boy." Rob slipped the wad of notes into the hand of the maître d' as Lee finished signing the account.

There was a chorus of thanks and goodbyes as everybody trooped through the lobby to their various conveyances. Lee turned to Natalie, saying, "Ride in our cab and we'll drop you."

"You always seem to be rescuing me from the wrath of my sitter."

Laughing Gus said, "Actually, I would like to pick your brain about a climate project."

"Not tonight I'm afraid, all you'd gather would be wine soaked cotton balls."

As the three of them squeezed into the back seat of a cab. Lee suggested, "Why don't you bring your little one and come to the house next Saturday for dinner?"

"Amy will be there, and she is a rather good cook," Gus put in.

Giving him another of her narrow-eyed looks Lee added, "I'm sure you would love to bake enough pies so that everyone can take one home."

Unfazed, Gus added, "Ben always comes over with Amy. He could pick you up."

"That would be wonderful."

Smiling, Gus got out and held the cab's door for Natalie. Waving goodbye as the cab drove off Lee said, "I didn't know she was gay."

"Does it matter?"

"To me? Of course not. In the family? It'll be tough for her."

As they were getting ready for bed Lee said, "Sorry honey, this night out has really put a dent in my study schedule. I'll have to read most of tomorrow."

"Will you need the car?"

"No. I've got all my books here and I can go online for anything else I need."

"Will it be OK if I drive up to the new settlement and visit Elder Luke?"

"Of course it will. You don't have to keep asking my permission."

"Sorry. I'm feeling a little overwhelmed by this evening's display of opulence. Did you see how much Rob tipped that guy?"

"No. But it would be at least two hundred dollars. Places like that don't give their best wines to just anyone."

"Mmm, a very expensive way to get drunk."

"I hope you're not too drunk," she said, slipping her hand down towards his waistband. Sinking onto the bed there was a pleasant interlude of lovemaking before they fell asleep entwined in one another's arms.

Chapter Twelve

The following Saturday, Ben arrived in the early afternoon with Natalie and her little girl. Gus helped bring in an assortment of toys and other necessities. Natalie laid down the sleeping girl. "What can I offer you?" asked Gus.

"A cup of tea would be nice."

"Come into the kitchen, we'll see if there is enough room on the stove for a kettle."

Amy, with an array of pots, pans, bowls and cooling racks spread all over every surface, said indignantly, "Of course we can make tea."

Somewhat overwhelmed, Natalie asked, "Can I help?"

"Nope. Ben, for his sins, is on duty as pot and bottle washer."

Ben stuck his head through the swinging door from the dining room and asked, "Can I have Gus for a minute? I need his help to get the table covers on."

"Covers?" Gus asked.

"Yes. There are several layers to protect against spills and knocks under a heavy damask tablecloth. Truly beautiful. And the cutlery is an exquisite pattern in silver."

"Lee doesn't like to use the china," Gus said anxiously. "She's afraid of breaking it."

"That's all right. I found some heavy-duty crockery with a workman's pattern. I suspect one of the teacups could be thrown and hit somebody's head without even chipping."

Pushing through the door, Amy brought in a tray of tea things. Natalie followed with a plate of biscuits.

"Yum, cookies," said Ben.

"Biscuits," corrected Amy with admiration. "Gus made them."

Gus put on a flat voice to say, "I'm bored with pies. Anyway, biscuits and cookies are much easier to carry home."

"Should I call Lee?" asked Amy.

"No." Gus shook his head. "She's rattling out the first draft of an essay. She'll come down when she's ready."

"Somebody else wants attention though," Ben nodded to a corner seat in the dining room where a sleepy six-year-old was regarding them inquisitively.

Picking her up Natalie exclaimed, "There's my big girl. Look Jesse, we have new friends."

"Oh gee, everything has caffeine, too much sugar or fat, what..." began Amy.

"No worries," said Natalie. "Can you grab my bag?" The two women were soon engrossed in a discussion of healthy snacks for children.

Amy and Ben disappeared back into the kitchen to continue making fine food. Soon mouth-watering aromas seeped into the dining room.

Anxiously Natalie asked Gus, "You're sure I shouldn't help?"

"No. They enjoy creating meals together. Perhaps I could do that brain picking now?"

"Won't the others want to be part of it?"

"Not really. We'll give them the executive summary later."

"Here you go Jesse, you can play with your tablet for a while." Catching Gus's expression, Natalie told him, "It has useful learning games on it and in this room there are far too many fascinating things that will not withstand Jesse's methods of investigation."

"We'll have to childproof a space for the next time you come."

"Virtually impossible, all this antique furniture and these delicate knick-knacks," Natalie informed him, then asked, "Do you want children?"

"Maybe, if I think there will be a habitable world for them."

"Hmm. For me, Jesse is an affirmation. My goal is to leave our children with a world they can live in."

"Uh. With the island project, I have a more limited goal. What we need to do is move the church, intact, across the sound, along nearly a hundred miles of highway, then halfway up a mountain."

"Is that all?" asked Natalie with a quirky smile.

"Yes." Gus completely missed the irony in her voice. "There are two houses that can be moved along the highway with regular permits because they only take up one lane."

"What about overpasses? How will you get under those?" Natalie asked, drawn in by his intensity.

"The houses 'll be fine. For the church we'll have the trucks drive up the off ramp then down the on ramp. Engineers have checked it for us, it's doable. The width of the church is the problem; we'll need two trucks side-by-side. That'll fill both lanes which is why the highway will have to be closed."

"Why does the community want the church so badly? Can't they build another one?"

"The building is the core of the community. During storms and floods, everybody took refuge there, together. Every wedding, baptism and funeral was held there, dances on Fridays, socials on Saturdays, school when boats couldn't get across the sound, daycare while harvests were brought in or dykes were shored up." Gus wound down.

"People will say things like 'Surely the spiritual life of the community is in the people not a building. Just build another church.'"

"Elder Luke , all the community leaders in fact, are afraid that without the same church, the community will lose its core."

"Like the church in Africville," said Ben from the doorway.

"Exactly."

"Africville?" asked Natalie.

"Black community in a port back east. It died when its church was razed. I was sent in to ask if you want anything?"

"Cookies," pipped up Jesse without even looking up from the tablet.

"More tea, if it's not too much trouble" said Natalie apologetically. Pulling a notebook and pen from her bag, she said to Gus, "The key is closing the highway, right? How long would it need to be closed?"

"Not sure. Our fear is that we might shake the whole thing to pieces. Plus, two trucks driving in tandem will have to go slowly."

"OK. How slowly?"

"Four or five miles an hour, perhaps slower on hills, ramps and such."

"So, a day."

"Or more."

"To get the highway shut down, we'll have to coerce the government. That will take a very large, very wide, coalition of arm-twisters."

Jesse scowled at her tablet moaning, "Maaaum!" Natalie laughed and turned to help her daughter.

Ben returned with another tray of tea and biscuits. "Is she baptised?"

"I thought about it. I have faith rather than..."

"If, at every christening, across the country, the pastor, minister or priest offered up a prayer that future generations of the island community would be baptised in the church of their forebearers, that might get you some attention," suggested Ben.

"Elder Luke has been wondering what to do about that," Gus said thoughtfully. "The community will be going back to the island church for baptisms for the next few months."

"Maybe for weddings and funerals as well," suggested Ben.

"Record church events and post them to social media," said Natalie.

"I'm not that good with social media," Gus said.

"I am," Amy chimed in from the dining room door.

"Environmental Watch has cameras and editing facilities you can use."

KILLING OUR GRANDCHILDREN

"I can do release forms and find pro bono lawyers for any legal work I can't do," said Lee who, unnoticed, had come downstairs.

"I'm pretty sure Environmental Watch would put resources into this because it is climate change destroying a community. EW could work on media coverage."

"You don't look very optimistic, Natalie."

"It's one thing to click 'Like' but another to get a government to take action."

"Yeah, think of all the indignant cartoons that come out every year when we put the clocks back or forward an hour. No government ever does anything."

Nodding, Natalie went on, "One-on-one contact is becoming the only thing that works. Petitions, letter-writing and email campaigns have all become forms of protest, which elected officials ignore."

"How about an appeal from Elder Luke ? Something like 'Please visit your elected official and advocate for the highway to be closed.'"

"A mass appeal on the vid channels will only work if it's followed up by individual contacts."

"Then we get contact lists and send out an email."

"No," sighed Natalie. "Won't work. Each contact has to be personal, with content like 'Dear Jane, Pastor Jones gave me your contact information. I understand that you were one of the stalwarts who raised the money to re-shingle the roof of your church. The island community would greatly appreciate your help in convincing politicians to...'"

"Every letter?" Amazed, Amy asked, "You mean, the next letter would need to be 'Dear Mr. Brown, Mrs. White from your church social committee...'?"

"Yes. Thousands of people would have to go and see their representative."

"Who has contact lists like that?" asked Lee.

111

"Churches do," Gus replied. Lee gave him a startled look. He shrugged.

"Environmental Watch doesn't have the resources to do the contacting part of a campaign. That's why our most important criteria for taking on a campaign is volunteer involvement."

"Could the island community people do this?" asked Ben.

Gus shook his head. "Right now, they're living two or three families in a house while they build the rest of the community. Might get the school kids to do it as a media project."

"That could work. 'Live video chat with the children of the island church.'" Natalie bent over to pick up the tablet Jesse had abandoned when she moved on to a building block toy.

"We need a catchy name for this campaign."

"Ben, I need your help or we'll be having a burnt offering," Amy called from the kitchen, "Everyone else to the table, dinner is imminent."

Conversation moved to many topics as a magnificent meal was consumed.

"I'll need larger pants if I keep eating like this," said Ben, loosening his belt by a notch.

"You could take up marathon running with Amy," Gus suggested.

Amy looked up at him and said, "I'm easing back on that. I still like to run but I'm never going to make an Olympic team or anything like that."

"You cook good," stated Jesse.

Amid the laughter Ben assured Amy, "You'd make a great chef!"

"Aren't there programs where you can train as a sous chef?" asked Lee.

"Actually, I'm thinking of transferring into food sciences. What I'm really interested in is nutritional meals made with ingredients from local sources. The program I'm looking at has that specialization."

"The island community does that just because of their isolation. I'll take you to meet some of their cooks if you like."

Pouring more coffee Lee said to Ben, "Thanks for taking such good care of the table."

"The artisan in me appreciates the work it would take to make this table. Can you imagine the Sunday dinners that were held around it?"

"'Sunday Closure,' that's what we could call the campaign."

"Uh uh," said Natalie. "Too many negative connotations with business closures and loss of jobs. I like 'Island Church.' Probably not unique but unusual, neutral. Whatever you call a campaign the ether always dubs it something. You'll have no control over that."

Yawning, Jesse looked up from the corner seat where she had been playing. Natalie turned to look after her.

"You two take her home," Gus said. "We'll do the dishes."

Amy looked worried. "We did some of the pots but..."

"Go. We can do dishes, even pots," said Lee.

"Hey," Gus said, "you got one of her looks. I thought I was the only one who got those."

"For that you're doing the rest of the pots," Lee said.

After making up care packages for their friends, saying goodbyes and promising to be in touch soon, Gus and Lee set to work on the dishes. Later, once the dishwasher was running and the worst of the pots were soaking, they took the remains a bottle of wine and fell onto their bed. Lee flipped through channels looking for a half hour's light entertainment.

Finding a talk show she liked, she settled down to watch.

"Can I borrow the car again tomorrow?" he asked.

"Only if you promise to just tell me you're taking it next time."

"Uh. OK."

She looked at him then muted the television. "What's going on?"

"Thinking about the church campaign."

"You're sure the government wouldn't close the road for you?" she asked hopefully.

Gus shook his head, "No chance. Elder Luke asked. In fact, last year, we made a whole presentation showing it would only need to be closed between interchanges for a few hours at a time."

"I can't help with the pressure campaign."

"I understand about disqualifying you for the bar and everything."

"It's not that. I just don't have time. In fact, I'm relieved you're going up to the island community tomorrow because I am nowhere near finished my essay."

"Something will work out," he murmured as he bent down to kiss her. She clicked off the TV.

Sunday afternoon, Gus was back from seeing Elder Luke and whistling as he put together lunches and meals for the week. Lee came into the kitchen with an armload of dirty cups and plates. He broke off to ask her, "Essay done?"

"Thankfully." She began to load the dishwasher, saying, "I take it things went well."

"Very well. By happenstance, there was an island community meeting this afternoon. They thought a 'resurrection' theme might work."

"That won't offend people?"

"They don't think so." Gus made an openhanded gesture. "They ought to know better than I do. Elder Luke gave me contact lists from their online fundraising."

"Really. Online fundraising?"

"Yeah, I was surprised too. I thought they were electrolytes..."

"Electrolytes?" she quirked an eyebrow at him.

"Yeah, like luddites only electrolytes know nothing about computers, electronics or the internet. But no. You know that guy who goes around setting up free internet access for folk in rural communities? Yeah, well, he hooked them up. The teacher says she can get the kids to contact communities all over the world, so at least we can get a campaign started."

"Who's going to do all that work contacting people?"

"I'll start. On Tuesday I'll begin working with heavy machinery in the port so I can go over to EW after work each day. I'll get Natalie to set me up and I can write contact emails for a couple of hours."

"What are you doing with your big yellow machines, in the port?"

"Clearing and deepening drainage ditches, which is supposed to stop flooding in the spring. Also, it will be good training with the backhoe." At her baffled look he said, "You know, the big claw things," demonstrating with his hand. She gave him an 'Oh' look and finished with the dishwasher, then began washing her hands. He added, "Don't worry, I'll still be home in time to cook dinner."

That comment earned him a splash from the tap. Gus was about to retaliate when she shushed him and turned up the sound on the computer's livestream of the news. She listened intently for a minute. Then she explained, "They've moved the pipeline opening to the week before Christmas."

"Is that the one up north with the new pumping station? Supposed to increase the volume of oil coming into the port?"

Through tightened lips, Lee said, "Yeah, the opening date was supposed to be the end of November. Organizing was well under way for a large demonstration to get more environmental impact studies before it is allowed to open. It will be hard to mobilize people for a demonstration so close to Christmas."

She continued talking but Gus had tuned out. A splash of water brought him back. "I was saying, I suppose I'll have to humble myself to Father and fly with him up to the ranch for Christmas Eve."

"It's not like your weight will increase the fuel consumption," he said in mock consolation. "Well, not much anyway."

Whereupon he got another face full of water and the fight was on. Later, sides aching with laughter, they settled down to eat. "Maybe that colour-bombing guy could put in an appearance," suggested Lee with a mischievous look.

"Hmm," a mouthful of sweet potato gave Gus an excuse not to answer.

Chapter Thirteen

A few days later Gus locked his bicycle to a lamppost and walked the last few blocks to a workshop rental business. Entering the office, he saw a tough-looking middle-aged man seated behind the counter and asked, "So how does this work? I've never rented a workshop before."

"Easiest way to explain is to show you." Over his shoulder he called, "Hey honey, watch the counter. I'm going to show this guy a unit." Taking a bunch of keys the man said, "I'm Kendrick, the owner. Follow me."

"These units look pretty large, " observed Gus

Kendrick led him down a broad access road explaining as he went, "Yeah, people work on semis out here. That's why the access is so wide." Turning down a laneway, the owner went on, "Most of the units are wide enough for a single garage roll-up door and a regular door. You use your own locks and keys. I don't hold keys. That way I can't open your space up for anyone. Cops want in, they gotta break the locks off."

"The units are the size of a regular garage?"

"Some are. The one I'm going to show you, it's the only one available now, is the size of two garages behind one another. Here." The owner stopped, unlocked, then pushed up what looked like a typical garage door except high enough for a tractor-trailer cab.

Gus looked at the doors and commented, "Heavy duty."

"Prevents a lot of problems with break-ins. Somebody wants in, they're going to have to bring bolt cutters or a cutting torch."

"Is there any security?"

"Nope. You can get in twenty-four seven. Office is open during regular business hours, Monday to Friday. You pay cash or set up an automatic withdrawal for once a month." Gus found a light switch and flicked it. Nothing happened. "Hang on," said the owner. Finding another key on his ring, he unlocked the handle on a power box. Pulling the handle down then up again, he turned and said, "Try it now." The lights came on and Gus walked around the space, looked at the benches and a large sink with extra taps.

"You can have the benches if you want them. There are heavy duty plugs for stoves, driers or machines over there," the owner said pointing. "Cold water only. There's a couple of drains in the floors. Don't let anything toxic go down there or we'll have government inspectors all over us and you'll be very unpopular with the other tenants."

"Uh-huh. How come there are no windows?"

"Some units have them. Through there is the street," said the Kendrick, nodding to the back of the unit. "Less break-ins with walls."

Gus looked around thoughtfully for a minute. *As good as you're going to get.*

Impatiently, the owner asked, "So you want it or not?"

"Yeah, I'll take it. You said cash is OK, right?"

"I need a name and a phone number for the records. Come on down to the office and we'll get you set up."

For a couple of weeks Gus walked or rode through the roads and alleys around the workshop. Day or night, most of the units were quiet, so he guessed they were used for storage.

One Saturday, Gus rented a cargo van from a repair shop for cash and no questions. He spent the day touring the port, picking up supplies while pretending to be a home renovator. Late in the evening, he rolled into the almost deserted workshop rental place. After offloading his supplies, he retuned the van and shoved the keys through a mail slot.

Arriving home, Gus was surprised to find Lee curled up on the bed watching a movie. "Hi. Thought you were going up to the pumping station."

"Not enough people. We cancelled and spent the time organizing a small group who could make a firm commitment to go up in December."

"Pretty crummy day, huh?"

"Yeah. Come and make it better for me."

"I'd better shower first. I need to scrub off all this crud."

She clicked off the TV and rolled across the bed. "Well, I'll just come and make sure you do a good job."

The next morning Gus was making French toast and watching the livestream of a Sunday talk show when she came downstairs. Pouring herself a cup of coffee, with an appreciative "Yum," she went to see if the Sunday papers had arrived. Returning to the table with an armload of newsprint, she began to skim through the national news sections. He set cutlery, plates, a platter of crisp bacon, the coffee pot, cream, another platter with French toast and a jug of maple syrup on the table. By the time he sat down, she had absent-mindedly crunched her way through most of the bacon.

He snagged a couple of rashers before she got them all, commenting, "You're going to have terrible heart problems in middle age."

"If the world lasts that long."

"Oh. A new excuse for gluttony. Why worry, the world won't last that long."

"Am I getting fat?" she asked apprehensively, running a hand over her waist.

"Not that I noticed. 'Course the amount of peddling I do back and forth makes me so lean I'm hardly a fair comparison."

"Yeah. Hours on hours in a library chair makes me yearn for some movement."

"Um," he asked, "What did you want to do today?"

"Well, I know we're trying to keep Sunday's for 'us' time but..." she paused, then with a look of consternation continued, "organizing the protest is going to eat up time. I was hoping to use today to get ahead of next term's work..." Lee's voice trailed off.

"Uh huh, so you want to sit, your flabby self, down in the library rather than spend an invigorating day with me in the great outdoors."

"I don't really want to, especially if you're going to call me flabby."

"Tut. You know I'm not serious. If they weren't so expensive, I'd recommend one of those walking desks. It's supposed to pour down rain all day, and I have some indoor stuff that needs doing, so no problem."

"Wanna meet downtown for a movie and dinner?"

"I would but I'm going to be kind of messy, not to say filthy dirty."

"OK. That movie we missed at the theatre is being streamed already and we can order in."

"That works. About six?" Gus asked, as he began loading the dishwasher.

Putting cream and syrup into the fridge Lee paused for a minute, then said, "I might be a little late."

They walked to the bus stop together. Once on-board Lee began reading and Gus stared out the bus window, deep in thought.

Feeling her stand, he started to turn and she gave him a quick peck on the cheek. "My stop. See you later." Gus smiled in reply, appreciating the way she never asked him where he was going, or what he was doing. Lawyer training, he supposed. A few stops later, he stepped down from the bus and began the evasive routine he thought of as 'zigzagging,' through streets and alleys. Wondering whether he really needed all these precautions, he paid another cash fare for a different bus to take him in the direction of his new workshop. After switching buses a second time, and some more rambling around, he walked through the facility's gate. As he unlocked his shop door, he thought, 'No cameras but a single gate.' *Pretty easy to track your comings and goings.*

After building a partition to block the view into his space through the access door, Gus sorted supplies and checked machinery. Finally, he set to work with some colourful sheets of seed paper which he cut into two-inch-wide strips. Next Gus used water-soluble glue to paste the strips together end to end, so he had a streamer about twenty-five feet long.

As soon as the glue dried he began experimenting with getting the strips to drop out of his ammunition canisters. At first the rolled streamers just fell out of the tubes in a lump. He put a weight on the end of the streamer but it pulled the glued strip apart. *Trial and error.* 'Too much error.' After several more modifications, he could toss a cannister up into the air and have the glued strips fall out in a long stream. *Most of the time.* 'Enough for today.' He left early enough to pick up Thai takeout and get warmed up with a shower before Lee got home.

That week, the weather turned to a cycle of slushy snow followed by cold rain. The drainage ditches filled with runoff and all manner of garbage. Gus did not mind because he was learning the tricks of clearing blocks and stopping overflows. Wednesday, as Gus was riding to Environmental Watch, there was a letup in the rain, so he detoured to check his rental mailbox. He was surprised to find a letter amongst the catalogues and flyers. As he stepped outside, it began to rain again, so he tucked the letter into an inside pocket to keep it dry and pedalled off to the EW office.

At the back door, Gus locked up his bike and got himself buzzed in. Immediately, he stripped off his rain gear and hung it amongst many other sets of outerwear. Natalie arrived with a towel and a steaming cup of coffee.

"An angel of mercy has appeared," he joked, scrubbing the water from his face and drying his hands.

"How is the church emailing going?" asked Natalie as she exchanged the towel for the coffee.

"OK. Thinking up a different comment for every email gives my creativity a workout, but I'm sending ten or more emails every time I come in. I expect a lot of them are getting lost in the Christmas rush. A follow-up in January will be needed."

"How's the response?"

"Pretty good. People are supportive, some pastors promised to talk to their congregations, other parishioners are asking committees at their church to support the campaign. A couple have actually gone to see their local politician. People are sharing contact lists so I have lots more to do."

"Do you emphasize 'resurrection'?"

"Well," he looked abashed, "I'm not comfortable calling it that so it tends to come out 'island community church.'"

"I wouldn't be either. We'll have to come up with something shorter for a tag." Gus looked at her inquiringly. "Like a keyword. Something distinct like initials that we can put into video titles, blog posts or messages so that all of it will come up in people's searches."

"I don't think 'ICC' would be very catchy." He gestured toward a workstation. In response to Natalie's nod, he set down his cup and pulled his fleece over his head. Feeling something in a pocket, he pulled out a damp, crumpled letter.

"You've got mail," said Natalie with a smile.

"Looks like somebody used one of those water-soluble pens." Taking the moist towel from Natalie he said, "I'll lay this on top of the dryer while I put the towel in. Hopefully, I'll be able to read it later."

Returning to the workstation, he settled down to composing 'Please support moving the island church' emails. Natalie came by, dropped the dried letter down beside him, and said teasingly, "Don't forget your fan mail."

If there had ever been a return address on the envelope, it had washed off. The letter was written on the kind of fragile paper favoured by Europeans for airmail letters. The purple writing was smudged and full of little curleycues. His brows knitted as he tried to read it. Walking over to Natalie's space, Gus handed her the letter and asked, "Can you make this out?" He looked over her shoulder adding, "The writing seems to have a lot of those little hearts instead of dots and that sort of thing."

"No. It's a European cursive. Dutch, I think. The paper is so crinkled and the ink has smudged so badly I can't decipher much of it."

"What's this?" he asked pointing.

"Might be an email address. Looks like all lower case, 'g-e-m-m-a-j' at..." Natalie squinted at the page, "umm 'enviro' then maybe dot 'e-v-e.' Might be a European domain name, there are a lot of small activist networks over there."

"Hm. Can't imagine what it is, but I'll try the address and see what happens. Thanks Nat."

Gus sent a 'Hello, got a letter, maybe this isn't even you' email to the 'gemmaj' address. After putting in another half hour of emailing, he called goodnight to Natalie, pulled on his damp rain gear and set out for home.

Coming in from the garage, Gus again shed his rain gear and hung it to dry. Looking forward to a hot shower, he picked up his daysack and headed toward the bedroom. At the base of the stairs, he heard an odd swishing sound. Hoping nothing was broken, he ran up the stairs. The swishing was coming from Lee's workroom. Puzzled he knocked on the door.

"Come on in." He pushed open the door and gasped in amazement. There she was, walking along on a treadmill with a complete computer setup and bookstand in front of her. Lee grinned at him and said, "You're right. I'm going to feel much better using this every day, and the workstation means I won't lose any study time at all."

Gaping, he asked, "You can afford that?"

"Oh yeah. No problem. I called this morning, put it on the family account, left the library early, the guys came this afternoon and set it up. Hey presto, here it is. I'm really going to enjoy it." She stopped the machine, stepped off and gave him a sweaty kiss. "Time for a shower."

"Me too," said Gus, following her toward the bedroom.

Lee grinned over her shoulder. "Oh goody."

Chapter Fourteen

As the new date for the oil pumping station protest got closer, Lee got busier. A week of heavy slushy snow gave Gus a chance to practice with snowplows. The plow blades had to go up and down without hitting lampposts which was hard enough, but when the students were loaned out to help in rural areas, learning how to miss mailboxes was hair-raising. One Friday night, he got home late after a grueling day.

Lee was thumping along on her new toy when he stuck his head into her workroom. Giving him a grin, she reached to turn off the workstation and stop the treadmill. "What," he said with feigned relief, "no complaints that I am late and dinner is ruined?"

"Too worried about Crows to care. Anyway, I can put in an order for Thai while you shower."

"Crows. What kind of trouble are they making now?"

Bitterly she said, "They've latched onto the pumping station protest. Apparently they have nowhere else to go for Christmas, so they might as well get arrested and spend it in a nice warm jail cell."

"I don't get it. They bring their own lawyers. Why will it affect you?"

"Crows almost always turn the protests violent, then some of our people get sucked in, or the cops just take the opportunity to arrest, photograph and fingerprint some of our people that they don't have on file."

"You're flying out with your father the following Monday. Will you be able to make it?"

"Fortunately, he has business meetings all day. Arraignments will be Monday morning, so I should be back in time. If not, he can abandon me or wait. His choice. That new sci-fi flick is streaming. Go shower."

As Gus was coming out of the shower, he heard the doorbell ring. By the time he got to the basement rec room, she had opened a couple of beers and laid out the Thai food.

"That was a very quick delivery for Friday night," he commented.

"I tip well," she said offhandedly.

"The perks of privilege," he said, loading up a plate.

She looked at him askance. "You mean, like my family?" Lee's eyebrows went up with disbelief, as she continued, "No. Anybody who tips well gets faster service."

"You think just anybody can get a high-end exercise machine delivered the same afternoon?"

"Well. Yeah, I see your point, but I put that on the family account. Our account is probably flagged for immediate attention, but this is just a run of the mill Thai take-out place."

"I'm pretty sure your father has a security company minding you."

"What's that got to do with it? Besides, he's already got George on his payroll."

"No garden in the winter."

"George still shovels the snow and stuff," she said absentmindedly, then with a startled expression, "Really? But why would my father want information from a restaurant? And how would he get it?"

"If this were an action-adventure novel, a couple of operatives from the security company would bribe people working at the Thai restaurant, and other places, to give them regular reports on you. Someone in every restaurant, store or salon that you frequent."

"I don't go to salons," she said distractedly. "I'm having a hard time believing this," Lee added, picking at her food.

"Look on the positive side. Your father loves you; he doesn't want you hurt, kidnapped or arrested because that would impede your career."

"He'd be more worried about damaging his reputation because he wouldn't pay kidnappers to get me back." Pausing, she thought intensely for a moment then said, "I'm nowhere near the protests. I stay close to the jail. I just help people with the legal stuff."

"Anybody with you?"

"Somebody local usually drives, so I have hands free for note taking."

"Do you know them?"

"Not really. They're usually somebody local, from one of the smaller organizations."

"Are they always men? Do they seem a little older, in better shape, better drivers than the average protester?"

"Horse dung!" She scowled at her plate for a while, then stared at the wall as if it were not there. "How long have you thought this?"

He picked up the remote, clicked on a music feed and cranked up the volume. Turning to her, he spoke softly, "Seems possible this place is bugged. Let's go for a walk."

She looked at him aghast, then strode towards the stairs. Going up into the front hall, she grabbed a coat and slammed the door on her way out. Gus followed, picking up Lee's daysack, some gloves and a hat for her. He checked he had his keys and wallet, then turned off the lights, went out, closed the door and locked it. He could see her as she passed under a lamp post far down the street, striding with the energy of pure rage. Gus jogged after her.

Catching up, he silently paced along beside her. After quite some time Lee asked in a strangled voice, "What do you know, and how long have you known it?"

He shook his head and mimed phone. Scowling, she dug out her cell phone. He took it from her, expertly opened the back, slid out the battery and the SIM card. "Got a handkerchief or something?" Taking off her silk scarf, she offered it to Gus who quickly wrapped the phone so that its parts were muffled and gave it back to her, "Got anything else electronic on you? Car remote, beeper, electric door keys?

She shook her head, signaling 'no'. Taking her daysack she said, hesitantly, "In here are my library, credit and bank cards."

"Those are OK, I think. To answer your question, in the summer, once we got to your family 'cottage' I began to think about it." Lee watched him, as he continued, "There was a guy who got off the bus when we did, then he disappeared, as soon as Jimmy arrived with the van."

"I don't remember that."

"I try to notice things like that, in case somebody is looking for me. It was the same guy who liked to show off his muscles, tossing the bales around at the work site."

"Didn't he move into the tent next to us, with that girl? The busty brunette that I thought had eyes for you. I can't remember her name."

"Yeah, that's the pair."

"You think she was a...a what?"

"Minder, if you like spy novels. Most people would call them bodyguards."

"And you also think there are bugs in the house?"

"Makes sense. While you're out at school there's lots of time to install and maintain microphones and cameras. Then get a house across the lane or something; somebody could sit there and monitor you twenty-four seven."

"Offspring of nothing holy!" Furiously Lee proclaimed, "I'm going on a spending spree. After that nothing else goes on the family account. I'll get my own security and an electronic monitoring company to clear out all the bugs."

"I wouldn't. It'll just make your father's security firm suspicious. They'd probably try to infiltrate any personal security you set up."

"Frack, double-frack dipped in dinosaur dung." She clenched her fists. Through gritted teeth, she said, "Those bugs have to go. Thinking people are watching me, or listening to me, all the time gives me the creeps."

"Set up electronic interference with the signal."

"How do you mean?"

"Well. I had a discreet look for wires when I first moved in but I couldn't find any. I'm pretty sure the bugs have some sort of radio link.

That means you should be able to set up some new electronic device, like, say a satellite dish, with what looks like a modem but actually jams the signal from the bugs."

"Who would know about that kind of tech?"

"Maybe Natalie? Environmental Watch must have these kinds of issues."

Seeing that she had calmed down, he handed her the gloves and toque. Pulling on the hat, she stopped dead in her tracks and stared at him. "Is this a danger to you?"

"Well, we're not out here on the street because I want a surveillance team to know my every thought." A smile crinkled around his mouth. "But I have long known not to make any offhand comments to anybody. Sure, your father's people could follow me, and find out things that I don't want anyone to know, but that's not really a danger. I'm very careful."

They came up to a main road and Lee put her fingers in her mouth to make an ear-splitting whistle. A taxi jerked to a stop beside them. Gus's questioning look got an explanation from Lee. "I have visions of my father listening to tapes." She climbed into the cab, gave the driver directions, then said to Gus, "The family has accounts at the ritziest hotels in the port. We're going to order champagne, oysters and the most expensive things on the menu. I'm going to get the boutique owner called in, so I can buy lots of clothes. It's all going on the family account. Tomorrow morning, I'll show up at the protest's legal team meeting in the most la-di-dah outfit you ever saw. After that, I'll take Rob to lunch, at his favorite restaurant, so I can pick his brains. You and I are going to go to a different hotel every night until I get the house debugged."

"Good thing I turned out the lights," he said mildly.

A couple of hours later, Lee was trying on clothes and talking into a pre-paid cell phone that she had bought on the way to the hotel. "Yes, tomorrow morning."

She held the phone away from her ear and regarded herself in the mirror. To the boutique owner she said, "Get your seamstress to do the hems. Don't worry about the waist for now."

Putting the phone back to her ear she said, "I know it's a week and a half before Christmas. You're a partner for crying-out-loud. I want you, your best contracts lawyer, the bank manager, the fund manager, stenographers, typists and a notary public." Holding the phone away from her ear again, she said to the boutique owner, "I'll pay your seamstress double her usual fee, in cash. I'm going to need shoes; can you help with that?" Scrunching the phone under her shoulder, she stepped out of the skirt, "Yes. I'm listening."

The boutique owner took the skirt, checked the size of Lee's trainer, gathered up some other clothes that needed alterations, mimed returning soon and left the suite. Gus looked on in amazement. Finally, he got a tonic water from the mini-bar and turned on the immense plasma screen TV. He flipped around until he found a news channel.

"Right. Eleven o'clock tomorrow at your office." Listening for a moment, she rolled her eyes and snapped, "I don't care what it costs." Disconnecting, she immediately dialed again, pacing while the phone rang. Finally, someone picked up and she said, "Hey Julia, I need to talk to Rob." She listened for a second then said, "I'm sorry. It's urgent. Please wake him." She began pacing again.

Gus got up and let in the boutique owner, who was carrying a stack of shoeboxes. Lee came over and watched as the shoes were unpacked. Pointing to a pair, she slid her foot into it and smiled gratefully at the excellent fit. Nodding her head, she called, "Honey, have you got any cash?"

"Uh. Yes."

"Give her fifty dollars would you?" Not noticing Gus's incredulous expression, Lee spoke into the phone. "Rob." She listened for a second then said, "No I didn't realize it was that late. Sorry, but I need to have lunch with you tomorrow." Listening again, she cut him off, "Not on the phone. One o'clock. I'll get Miguel to give us one of the back booths." Pausing for a little longer, she added, "I'm truly sorry. Please give Julia my apologies. Good night."

She slammed into the couch beside Gus, drummed her fingers madly on the cushions, then hopped up and began marching back and forth. Gus waited, sipping his tonic water and watching the weather report. Eventually Lee settled down beside him. "I forgot to ask," she said contritely. "Are the clothes you're wearing OK for tomorrow?"

"You don't want me to go back to the house?"

"Not until I get it debugged." With her impish smile she added, "I read spy novels too, you know."

"I'm not sure the 'Scarlet Pimpernel' is applicable to modern times." Lee swatted him. Glad to see her usual good humour returning, Gus went on, "No worry about the clothes. How long, before you'll be comfortable with moving back into the house?"

"Oh, probably a couple of days. I'll buy one of those small electronic security start-ups tomorrow. Hopefully, they can assess on Sunday, install some sort of jammer on Monday, so we can go home at the end of the day."

"Buy a security company?"

"Hmm," she answered, taking a sip from his glass. "That's why I need to talk to Rob. He worked in tech as a teenager."

"Buy a security company?" he repeated.

She looked at him, puzzled. "Sure. One of those two person start-ups working out of somebody's dining room. Shouldn't cost more than a million or so."

Gus looked at her astounded. "Mind if I ask you a question?"

"How much money do I have? I don't know. That's why I'm getting the lawyers and whoever together tomorrow. For too long, I've just let my father 'mind the store.' I'm going to get everything put under my direct control. Ask me again tomorrow evening, I should know how much I'm worth by then."

"Okay," he said, shaking his head in wonder, "but I have a question about tipping the boutique owner fifty dollars, in cash. Smaller than peanuts, I know, but I'm curious."

"You think I should have given her more? Oh, I'll give you back the fifty." She started to get up.

"Relax. I'm not worried about the money. I just wonder why you gave her cash. Didn't you put a tip on the account invoice you signed?"

"Of course. Oh, I see. Always give a cash tip, no matter what you add electronically. They can't hide the amounts in electronic transfers but the cash can go straight into their pocket. My father taught me that." Musing she added, "He's not always wrong."

Yawning he asked, "Ready for bed?"

"Are you really tired?"

Chuckling, he answered, "Not that tired."

"Oh goody."

Waking to the sound of Lee's voice, Gus squinted at the clock. Barely five-thirty. Yawning and stretching, he looked into the living room area of the suite. Lee was striding back and forth, hotel bathrobe flapping wildly. She stopped in front of the hotel's intercom. Reeling off a breakfast order, she was about to redial then added, "Make that two carafes of coffee. Now connect me to the concierge." Striding off again until a voice came through the speaker, she started to rattle off instructions, "I need the laundry I sent down earlier back by seven. Make sure the boutique woman gets my suit..." She listened for a moment then continued, "Great, send it up with the laundry." Pausing again she nodded impatiently. "Yes, yes. If I need anything I'll call." Stalking over to a laptop standing on a small desk, she slammed into the chair and began hammering on the keys.

Shaking his head in amazement at this hitherto unseen aspect of her personality, Gus turned to the bathroom. After a long hot shower, he wrapped himself in the hotel's bathrobe and went out into the living room area of the suite. Two of the national newspapers had arrived with breakfast. Lee was still pounding away on the computer. Gus took the jug of orange juice over to refill her glass. She nodded distractedly. He settled down to read the newspaper and consume an excellent breakfast, grateful for the extra coffee.

There was a knock at the door. Lee brought the laptop over and set it down by him, saying, "Look at these company profiles would you." Snatching her wallet from her daysack, she continued to the door. After signing and tipping, Lee turned back into the room with an armload of clothing. Sitting down opposite him, she opened an envelope that had been attached to her suit. Giggling, she read aloud, "Dear Ms., I have taken the liberty of including appropriate undergarments with your suit." Looking at him Lee said, "That woman will do well."

Gus responded, "Seeing that you got her out of bed in the middle of the night, she has been very obliging."

"She's used to dealing with Hollywood drama queens. I'm considerate by comparison."

"Yeah, I suppose. And you tip well."

"Always. I emptied your pockets onto the credenza before I sent your clothes to be laundered."

"Find anything interesting?"

"Nope," she replied, making a funny face at him. "Oh. That was a serious question, wasn't it? No, really not, just your keys and wallet. Can you take the stuff I don't need, and bring it to the Harbour Hotel tonight?"

"Boy when you go high end, you really go high end, don't you?"

"Oh, come on. It's a whole notch down from this place. But it has great views of the ocean."

"I wouldn't know. What time?"

"Probably around six."

Gus picked up his clothes and went to get dressed. Lee fingered a slip appreciatively then set out the suit, shoes and a clasp purse. Next, she packed everything else into a large shopping bag.

Gus returned and picked up the bag, "This everything?"

"Yes. Are you off?"

"Unless there's something you need," Gus said, retrieving the components of his phone from a drawer in the credenza. "You've got yours still disassembled right?"

With a rueful smile, Lee said, "Right. I'll have to improve my spy skills."

Kissing her, and smiling as he left, Gus said reassuringly, "Wouldn't worry. Even with your father's resources, he couldn't have gotten up on your burner phone this quickly. But if you're worried—switch to a new SIM card once a day or so. See you tonight."

Chapter Fifteen

Riding the bus, Gus thought about Lee's vehement fury at the violation of her privacy. He admired the way his wife had taken command of her situation. Startled he began to feel his way around the idea of Lee as a 'wife,' he knew, although they had never talked about it, that there was a deep current of love between them. Lee supported his actions without openly acknowledging them, while he applauded her intense belief in driving climate solutions through enforcing the law. They were fitting a life together, around the demands of their beliefs.

The bus jerked to a stop, shaking him out of his thoughts. Pay attention lover boy, or it will be a relationship through bars. Forcing himself to concentrate, Gus began hopping buses, interspersed with fast-paced side street walks. Eventually, he turned onto a street full of grungy auto repair garages. He cut across a front lot jammed with wrecks to enter a dirty white building. A man walked toward him, wiping his hands on a greasy rag.

"Thought you weren't going to make it."

"Huh. Giving you some extra time to finish the job," Gus replied, with a cocky grin that he did not feel.

"Oh sure, well, she's ready. Good chassis, drive train, motor, gonna need new tires soon. Body's a mess, but keep slapping fiberglass to it and it won't fall apart. Only real problem is the gearshift. It can take a couple of tries to get it from first to second to third. Fourth and fifth are OK."

"What about the four-wheel drive?"

"Seems OK, I ran it up and down a couple of muddy hills without problems. We agreed thirteen hundred dollars."

"Eleven hundred, but I'll make it twelve if it starts first try."

The mechanic snorted, and tossed Gus the keys. He fired up the big boxy vehicle and drove to the end of the road. Getting out, Gus checked the wheels and undercarriage, then ground around the muddy field for a while. Putting it back into two-wheel drive, he returned to the garage. Climbing down, he counted out twelve hundred and handed it to the mechanic, who counted it again. "Papers are in the glove box. Come back any time."

Gus went into a coin operated car wash and used a hand-held spray gun to thoroughly wash the car. Then he fed coins into a vacuum cleaner to make his careful examination of the car's interior seem normal. Fairly certain he was not carrying any GPS trackers in the big car, he drove to his workshop and backed in. Putting a couple of buckets of chickpeas to soak in bright lime green dye, he loaded everything else he would need to test his new multi-barrel air cannon into the cargo space. After a quick check of the shop, he locked up. Always arriving and leaving through the same gate still spooked him, so he hopped on a few extra buses as he wove back and forth across the city.

Upon arrival at the Harbour Hotel, Gus was informed by a clerk at the front desk that Lee had not yet checked in and had left no message for him. Realizing he had forgotten to get the number for her prepaid phone, Gus bought a coffee and a newspaper then settled into a lobby chair. After an hour, he realized the porters were keeping a wary eye on him. Lee's arrival in a bright red rain cape caused a minor commotion. Slipping a tip into the head porter's hand, she directed him to unload her taxi. When a bellhop headed toward the door, she called to him with a laugh, "You'll need a rack."

Putting on the airs of a debutant, she bounced across the lobby calling, "Sweetheart, you didn't have to wait down here for me." After giving him a passionate kiss, she asked, "What suite are we in?" Gus made an awkward gesture which caused Lee to turn to the front desk with a look of haughty disdain.

Rob came in and waited beside her at the registration desk, followed by the bellhop with an overloaded luggage rack. Gus went over and shook hands with Rob, who blew out a breath and said, "Haven't seen her like this for a long time."

"Does she get like this often?"

"Not since she left the sailing team." Giving him a sharp look, Rob added, "Lee could have been an Olympian, you know, probably would have won gold. She has this cutthroat ability to make things happen."

"Why'd she stop sailing?"

"On the International Circuit she saw the mess pollution was making of the oceans, especially plastic. Just stopped sailing and put all her energy into opposing polluters."

Lee turned with a dazzling smile, saying, "Off we go. Rob, come up for a few minutes, I need to sort some things out for you."

An obsequious manager led them to an express elevator. The bellhop followed in a freight elevator. Doors were opened, help with unpacking was waved away, tips were dispensed and the door to the suite was closed. Lee plumped down on a couch and kicked off her shoes exclaiming, "What a day!"

Gus found the mini-bar and pulled out a bottle of white wine. He cocked an eyebrow at her.

"Yes please."

"What about you Rob?"

"Is there any decent whisky in there?"

After squinting at the bottles for a moment, Gus held up one saying, "How about this stuff with the blue label?"

"That'll do nicely, old man."

Taking a tonic water for himself, he brought the drinks over to the sofa. Sitting down, he stared out through the wall of glass at a beautiful ocean sunset. "How on earth did you get this room?"

"She's been doing it all day," said Rob, sipping his whisky. "Miguel wanted to give us a table at the restaurant's front window but she made him give us one of the booths in back, where businessmen have discreet meetings. Then she had him seat a couple of beefy fellows at the window. Not Miguel's idea of showing off suitable clientele."

"How did things go?" Gus inquired.

"Well, I didn't have it all my way, " responded Lee. "I arrived for the protest meeting at the advertised time, but of course, the Crows' lawyer was three quarters of an hour late. Fifteen minutes after that, I just got up and breezed out. EW's lawyer was a little startled. I'll have to make it up to him tomorrow." Standing up for a moment, she shucked off her suit jacket, undid her top buttons and pulled the tails of her blouse out of her skirt. Sitting down again, she took a long swallow of wine. "That's better. My lawyer and his entourage were a grumpy lot, especially when I told them what I wanted done. If the looks on their faces were any indication, their opinions of me ranged from spoiled brat to bat-dung crazy. Then, I told them the papers were to be ready for signatures by the time I got back from lunch and flounced out. Well not really, but you know. When I got to the front lobby, there were those two beefy guys that Rob mentioned." Looking at Gus she added, "Whom I wouldn't even have noticed last week. That made me think. I went upstairs again and marched back into the boardroom. I reminded them they worked for me, and if I had the slightest inkling that any of them had told my father about my changes, I'd fire all of them. Then I 'flounced' back out again." Overcome by a giggling fit Lee could not continue.

Rob took up the tale. "So once she got the seating at the restaurant arranged to her satisfaction, we had a wonderful lunch. As it happens, I did know the owner of one of the electronic security firms she was interested in. I gave him a call."

Catching her breath, Lee continued, "Back to my lawyer's office to sign the papers moving all my money and investments into my direct control."

"She had me witness them as well, which isn't technically necessary when you have a notary, but it makes the contracts a lot more difficult to break."

"Then, the electronics guy turned up."

"The two of them went into a closed-door meeting, and Lee left me with all those hotshot lawyers, whom she had forbidden to leave. We sat around staring at one another. Very uncomfortable, I can tell you."

"Good practice for your future career as a business magnet," said Lee. "Anyway, the electronics guy and I hammered out a deal pretty quickly."

"Then, she comes out, and tells the fund manager to liquidate a million dollars' worth of stocks."

"I didn't want those oil stocks anyway."

"Tells the lawyers and the rest of them to get a purchase agreement for the tech company drawn up for her to sign, when she comes back from shopping."

"Well, it was going to take them a couple of hours anyway, and I haven't had time to do any Christmas shopping," explained Lee.

"Usually, I can't stand shopping with women," said Rob, "but she's a whirlwind. I've never seen anyone buy so many presents, so fast."

"And, it was all on family accounts. You really were a sweetheart, Rob." Lee got up and began rummaging through the piles of parcels on the luggage rack. The suite phone rang, and she picked it up listened, then said, "Fine, send it up." Walking over to Rob she handed him a couple of boxes. "These are for Julia, tell her if the fit is not good or the colours don't complement her complexion, she should return them. The gift receipts are in there. The consumable is for you," she said, handing him a larger bottle of the blue-labeled whisky he was drinking. Rob gaped a bit then managed to stutter his thanks.

The doorbell rang; Rob took the opportunity to depart, while the bellhop lugged in a couple of large bags. Lee pointed at one and said,

"Gus, these are some work clothes for you. The tech guy is pretty sure he can solve our problem in time for us to go home on Monday."

Gus nodded. She joined him on the couch, and tucked her arm into his. They quietly sipped their drinks, and watched through the window as a panorama of colours settled into darkness.

Lee asked, "How was your day?"

"Sedate compared to yours. The bag of your stuff is on the bed. I hung up the clothes, but they'll probably need ironing or steaming or something," Gus watched the last of the colours fade away, then added, "Had a thought that gave me pause." Catching his tone, Lee looked at him expectantly. "Found myself thinking of you as my 'wife.'" She stilled and looked at him with some apprehension. "Yeah. Caught me by surprise too."

They sat silently for a while, regarding their reflection in the window. Presently she began speaking, "Well, after a couple of years we'll qualify as common-in-law spouses. If I were pregnant, most places would recognize the union immediately."

He looked at her in consternation, "Whoa. I wasn't even thinking about having children."

"No. Me either, I'm just saying that's the law."

Gus's voice wavered as he said, "The way things are going, in fifty years nobody will be able to live outside geodesic domes that have a life support system. I don't want to bring kids into that."

Upset, Lee spoke urgently, "No. No. I agree, no children until we are sure we will not leave them to be baked alive. It's only the legal part that bothers me. Until we are married, I can be compelled to testify against you."

"What you don't know you can't tell."

"True."

"And you don't want kids."

"Same as you. Not yet. Maybe never."

"OK. I love you. No complications."

"Well, not exactly."

Gus looked at her aghast, "You don't love me?"

"Of course, I love you. At least I think I do. I'm only twenty, and my family is not exactly a great role model."

"That's OK. Mine either. We'll carry on the way we have been and if... I mean..." Gus stumbled to a stop

"It isn't that at all. It's my family. Once we are married, in any way, including common-law, you will have rights to my money."

"There must be some legal document I can sign, saying I don't want any of it."

"But that's no good. If I were, you know, gone, I wouldn't want you to be poor."

"Wouldn't be the first time. Anyway, if I lost you, your money would be the least of my problems."

Lee put down her wine glass and wrapped her arms around him.

"You are a wonderful man. I do love you."

Chapter Sixteen

Early the next morning Gus slid out of the gargantuan hotel bed and turned on the weather channel with the volume very low. While he dressed, in some of the 'work' clothes Lee had bought for him, Gus paid close attention to the regional weather. He was glad to see that he would be able test fire the air cannons in clear dry weather. He slipped out of the suite, left the hotel, trotted down the road and hopped on a bus. He felt uncomfortable and wondered if it was the all-brown work clothes that made him look like he was delivering parcels or the babel of many languages spoken by a bus full of new citizens coming off the night shift.

As usual, Gus began switching buses and walking through side streets. As he arrived at his workshop, he felt a lingering sense of anxiety. *Fairly sure nobody followed you.* Grunting agreement with himself, Gus checked the chickpeas to make sure the dye had soaked in properly, then loaded them into his vehicle. He drove a zig-zag route to the highway, warily watching the rear-view mirror for unwanted followers.

Gus pulled his truck off the track near the loggers' shack and hid it behind some bushes. He took out the bucket of chickpeas and his new multi-barrelled air cannon, and trudged off down the trail, switching the bucket from hand to hand every hundred yards or so. *At least it will be empty on the way home.* At the shack, he stood quietly for a few minutes watching and listening. When he was satisfied that nobody was about, Gus continued along beside the little creek to the clearing where he would test fire his cannons. Settling himself just inside the trees, he pulled a cold lunch out of his daysack and ate with one eye on the clearing.

After lunch he set up his air cannons then took out the streamer canisters. Weighing one in his hand, not sure how well it would fly, he loaded two canisters of streamers and four of the chickpeas. Kneeling, he set the multi-barrel cannon across his leg, so that it sloped up at approximately forty-five degrees from the ground. Firing the first barrel, he watched with a smile as the canister arched into the air and dumped the bright green chickpeas all over his target area. Rotating to the second barrel, he fired a canister of streamer, but was disappointed. Halfway to the target, the container tumbled around in the air and dumped out one big roll, not streaming at all.

He spent a while trying different ways to load streamers into canisters, until eventually he was ready for another test fire. This time it worked fairly well, with the colourful paper shaking loose and floating out in the wind. After that Gus spent several hours modifying, loading and firing the rolls of paper, until he could get them to sail down like pennants at the ends of his target area. Next he practiced firing in rapid succession. Finally, convinced he could deliver four cans of lime green chickpeas and two colourful streamers, on target, in less than a minute, he packed up and went back to his vehicle.

Taking a couple of backroads, Gus entered the highway at a different junction than he had left it, and drove carefully back to the port. Once he got back to his garage, he set to work and vacuumed out the inside of his vehicle, then used his power hose to wash the outside, making sure all the gunk and mud went down the drain. Finally, Gus stripped off his fancy brown 'work' clothes and put on some everyday clothes he kept in a locker.

Even after the long day Gus, was still cautious and spent a couple of hours of zigzagging and bus-hopping his way back to the hotel. This time, the desk clerk was very attentive, giving him a key card, informing him there were no messages and that his 'wife' had returned half an hour earlier. Gus nodded his thanks and went up to the suite.

Letting himself in, he was tempted to call out 'Honey, I'm home,' but he walked through to the bedroom and found Lee in the shower. Gus watched for a few moments, until she saw him through the glass door and beckoned for him to join her, which he was happy to do.

Later, as they stood in front of the sinks, she pointed and said, " What's that?" He looked to where she had pointed, at the base of his thumb, and was startled to see a splotch of lime green dye on his skin. Appalled, his head snapped up to see a determined look on Lee's face, as she said, "You have got a bruise."

He paused for a second then said "Yeah. Are you going to let me watch the football game tonight?"

"Only if you promise to explain the rules to me."

"For a future lawyer, you sure have a hard time understanding a few simple rules."

"Ha. I ordered steaks and trimmings, should be sent up in about ten minutes, or would you like something else?"

"That's great," Gus said, opening the minibar and taking out a beer. He looked at her inquiringly, but she shook her head, and picked up a half empty glass of wine on her way to the couch.

"Busy week coming up. Most of the pro-bono lawyers can only make evening meetings. Then, the team is going up to a town near the demonstration site early Saturday, to get set up and be ready for Sunday. What is your week like?"

"Three A.M. standby every morning, in case a storm blows in. If it doesn't snow then we do maintenance on the trucks and plows. Expecting a ton of snow next week, so it will be long hours until after Christmas. Am I going to see you again, before you go to the ranch with your father?"

"Friday night. Even free lawyers like me don't work on Friday nights."

"OK, if it's snowing I'll pretend I broke my leg."

Laughing she said, "With a miraculous recovery by Saturday morning."

"Of course." They ate and watched some of the game, then went to bed.

Rising early, Gus checked the weather channel, and hustled out to the truck barn. He was reading the paper with his customary coffee and donuts as Joe and his other workmates trickled in. Since the snow had not started, they were able to leave at the end of their scheduled shift. Thankful that he had enough time, Gus went to his workshop where he got all the gear ready and loaded into his car.

As he plodded up the street, Gus was glad to see lights blazing from their house. The wreath on the door brought a smile to his face, and the sound of her machine clanking away made him bound up the stairs to poke his head through her workroom door, "All good?"

"Good as it can be."

"What do you want for dinner?"

"You," her eyes widened ridiculously, "but Amy left a casserole ready to heat up."

Half an hour later Lee joined him at the kitchen table to watch the news as they ate. After the weather report, Gus checked the weather network and looked at the overnight temperatures and radar map displays. "Looks like the snow'll get here tonight. Early to bed for me."

"No essays for me, so I'll join you."

For the next three days, Gus worked long shifts as the first heavy snowfall of the year blew into the port. Lee spent her days in the university library and her evenings meeting with lawyers, in anticipation of arrests at the pumping station protest. By Friday, they were both exhausted and settled for in an evening at home. He searched through the steaming services for a movie while she ordered in the ubiquitous Thai meal.

Lee told him, "We'll have at least three busloads for the pipeline demo, so it will be a decent showing. Not the huge event we had hoped for on the earlier date, but substantial."

"What about the Crows?" he asked.

"Eh. They operate as a self-contained unit, even down to using their own transport, so we don't know how many of them will show up.

We've recruited hard, amongst our more law-abiding, pacifist groups. That way, we hope to keep our people from getting caught up in whatever the Crows start."

"Getting much media?"

"Not a lot. Unlikely any actual journalists will trek up there with us. It would take too long." She added with a wry smile, "They need the time for all those feel-good, brotherhood of man stories."

"Pity."

"There's good cell reception." Lee continued, "We'll be able to put up a couple of live streams. That will give us some coverage, and help prevent it turning into a riot."

The doorbell rang and she went to pay for the delivery. Coming back into the kitchen, Lee stopped and looked at a brightly-wrapped package on the table. "What's this?"

"Figure I won't see you again until New Year's, so this is your Christmas present."

Putting down the food, Lee got the kitchen stepping stool and reached up into the back of a high cupboard to get a box wrapped in shiny red paper, with a frilly bow and a tag as big as a Christmas card. She gave it to him confessing, "I had it wrapped."

Keeping it in one hand, he took her into his arms. They embraced one another for a while, until gently separating, and she said, "You know what? Let's eat in the dining room tonight."

"You're not worried about the table?"

"What's the sense of having a beautiful table if we never use it?"

Spreading a double layering of the damask tablecloth at one end of the table, Gus found the china and candles while she set out the Thai food and found a fine bottle of white. As they ate and drank, they perused the books they had gifted one another. Lee read him rulings from the book of arcane common-law precedents and Gus responded by imitating the oration of great revolutionaries.

Chapter Seventeen

Jerking upright in the dark Gus groped around for his phone. He finally found it and grunted, "Yeah?" After listening for a moment, he answered, "I'm supposed to be off for the next two days." Again, the voice scratched out of the speaker, and finally he agreed, "OK. OK. It'll take me about an hour to get there."

Crawling out of the bed, he began searching in drawers for work clothes. Pushing herself up on one elbow, Lee asked in a sleep-fuzzed voice, "What's up?"

"I've got to go in."

"How come?"

"Joe had to take Dvora to the emergency."

She sat up and with a look of concern asked, "What's happened?"

"Maybe a premature birth. Hopefully, they're just being careful."

"Anything I can do?"

"Nah." He went over to the bed and kissed her lightly. "Go back to sleep. I'll see you at New Year's."

Stepping down the stairs as quietly as he could, Gus sat on the bottom step to lace up his boots and went outside into whirling wet snow. *Yeah and you'll leave tracks in fresh snow.* Gus pulled on his hat and gloves. He wondered if he would have to abandon his action. From the depot, Gus drove a snow plow into the storm. Several hours later, he brought it back in to refuel. The course supervisor came over to the pump and asked if there were any problems. Shaking his head, Gus said, "Just my girl's gonna put me in the doghouse for missing her party."

Laughing, his boss told him, "Do Route Six again. Clear skies are coming in. I should be able to release you in time to help put up decorations."

By midafternoon Gus was on the highway north. *Only six hours behind schedule.* Late in the afternoon, he filled his tank so that he would not need to get more gas until after the action. *If all goes well.*

As the light was beginning to fade, Gus turned off the highway, then onto a sideroad and finally pulled into what he hoped was the logging track that would take him into position. He got out with his map and compass to check his location. Satisfied that he was on the right track, he turned back towards the truck.

A few feet to his right a figure rose from the ground. Surprised, Gus managed to nod in greeting. The man moved in a way that made him seem like part of the land. His lined face was old, with sharp dark eyes peering out from under his creased brows. A younger man appeared at his shoulder and asked, "My grandfather wonders what you are doing on this land."

"I intend no harm, just want to do a little hiking."

"He says if you go up this track, you will come close to the pipeline."

"I didn't hear him say anything." The younger man looked at Gus steadily and waited. Not sure how to proceed, Gus continued, "I'm not going that far."

The older man regarded Gus with ferocious intensity. Finally, he tipped his chin to the younger man. "He says you should go up this track about seven hundred paces. You'll come to a clearing. That is a good place to stop. Don't go north from there or you hit the pipeline. The eastern trail leads to some easy walking country." The two men stepped back into the forest. Although he was looking straight at them, Gus could not see where they had gone.

Gus parked where he had been told; first light found him struggling out of his sleeping bag and into his boots. Overnight about six inches of snow had fallen. *Perfect for tracking.* 'Not likely the pipeline people will have trackers,' thought Gus as he pulled his gear out of the truck. He was about to close up when his eye caught on the snowshoes. *Might be deep drifts or more snow could come down.* He strapped the shoes onto his pack. Checking the map and compass, he took a bearing and set off through the forest and gullies. He made good time, and was moving so well that he almost burst out of the trees into the bare downhill side of a ridge. He supposed the oil company had clear-cut the area around the station for some reason of their own. *Gives you a clear shot at the platform.* Gus estimated the range at about seventy-five yards from the ridgetop. Scouting back and forth along the ridge, he found a depression in which he could lie down and still have a clear line of sight to the stage that was being set up at the pumping station. He shucked off his pack and leaned it against a nearby tree, then crawled up to the lip and settled himself in behind some bushes

At the bottom of the ridge, beside the buildings, the stage had been built around a double elbow of pipe that stuck up from the ground, like an inverted "U" with a big red wheel on top. Guessing that the dignitaries would all help to open the valve, he decided that would be the best target for his chickpeas. It was still some hours before the event, and the only people in sight were workers setting up a line of company flags. *Nice of them to put up wind gauges.*

The corporation was working hard to create a festive air with balloons and hot chocolate for kids. For several hours Gus lay shivering on the cold ground, watching enviously as folk were served hot coffee and donuts. At last, it looked as if the ceremony would begin. One of the corporate representatives stepped towards the mic just as three busses rolled up behind the crowd and disgorged a stream of protesters, who began chanting loudly in an effort to drown out the corporate message. The executive shrugged with a look that said, 'it is too cold for any shenanigans,' then moved toward the red wheel and waved for the other dignitaries to join him.

Gus slid back to pick up his multi-cannon and knelt ready to fire. As he lined up the first shot, he was startled by the rumble made by two flatbed trucks roaring up between the back line of the protesters and their busses. The Crows had arrived. In their symbolic black clothing, they jumped off their trucks to form a flying wedge, which charged towards the stage.

KILLING OUR GRANDCHILDREN

Demonstrators, children and townspeople were all shoved and trampled by the charging Crows. Accustomed to brawling, the local men were soon giving better than they got. Demonstrators and townsfolk alike protected children, getting them away from the Crows by picking them up and passing them, hand to hand, until they were out of harm's way. That done, the demonstrators struggled back toward their buses. Gus remembered why he was there and fired off a streamer, which worked perfectly and came down on the upwind side of the stage. In quick succession, he fired four loads of lime green chickpeas, which scattered across the stage, and then a second streamer on the downwind side of the stage. He watched as dignitaries splattered with lime-coloured splotches were hustled off the stage by security guards.

The brawl's distracting everyone. Move out. Ducking down, Gus moved quickly into the woods, catching up his pack as he went by. Using a steady careful pace, he ran down the hill. Just before he came out into the open, he halted under the cover of the branches and looked warily around. Seeing nothing to alarm him, Gus was about to set off when the old man rose up a couple of steps to his right. Startled, Gus managed not to cry out.

The old man tipped his chin at the snowshoes attached to his pack. Gus looked out through the trees and realized that while he had been up the ridge, a lot more snow had drifted into the gully. Nodding, he put the snowshoes on the ground and stepped into them, glad of the modern harness, which he could snap closed with one quick movement. Meanwhile the old man had set off along the gully on what looked like handmade, bear paw snowshoes. With his narrow, lightweight metal shoes Gus quickly started across the gully.

The old man stopped, shook his head and directed Gus down the gully with a chopping motion of his hand. Taken aback, Gus thought quickly, 'The car is parked across the ridge, why go down the gully?' *It's his ground, trust him.*

149

Gus followed the old man down the gully, doing his best to keep up. At last, they came out into a clearing. His car was parked up against the forest edge and the young man was leaning against it. Gus stood breathing hard.

"My grandfather says you shoe pretty good, for a city guy."

"Huh." Panting, Gus loaded his gear into the truck. He wondered how the young man had moved his truck but guessed there was no point in asking. "Where am I?"

"See the firebreak at the end of the clearing, follow it down to the gravel road, go to the blacktop and follow that to the big highway."

"Got it." Gus climbed up into the driver's seat.

"Grandfather says, do not worry about your tracks. We shot a deer. We'll carry the carcass home over your tracks. No one will know you were here."

Gus put the key in the ignition and started the car. The old man turned away and the young man followed him. Suddenly remembering, Gus slammed on the brakes, scrabbled through his daysack then jumped down and ran after the two men calling, "Wait!" When he caught up with them, he used both hands to offer a package to the old man. Bending slightly the old man took the pouch of tobacco.

The young man's lips quirked as he said, "Grandfather thanks you, for your efforts to defend the land."

Returning to his car, Gus looked over his shoulder but they had disappeared. On the drive back to the port, he listened to local news, which reported on the chaotic event at the pumping station with evident relish. A phone-in program got mostly callers who said things like, "It's a good idea to teach out-of-towners where they aren't wanted." Downcast, Gus drove on through another snowstorm.

Chapter Eighteen

Getting home that night was a long, hard trip for Gus. The drive back to the port got worse and worse as the storm dumped wet slushy snow onto the roads. Exhausted, he got the big boxy car into his shop, washed it down, stowed his gear, changed his clothes and headed out, only to realize his dismantled phone was still in the workshop. He zigzagged his way back to the shop, picked it up and headed for home again. Once he was within a few miles of home, he put in the SIM card and battery, which triggered a frenzy of texts and voice messages ringing and dinging their notifications.

First, Gus texted Lee's mobile, to say he was on-air and if possible could she please call or text. He waited a quarter hour, but got no reply, so he began backtracking through the texts, mostly demands to call in to work. Deleting those, he started on the voicemails and was concerned to hear Lee's voice coldly inform him, "We'll talk when I get back." None of the other voicemails or texts gave him any clue as to what was upsetting her. Getting off the last bus, he stumbled down his street in a dispirited daze.

Gus was struggling to open the front door when his phone rang again. In his eagerness to hear Lee's voice, he dropped his keys into the snow piled up on the porch. Instead of Lee, he heard his course supervisor growling at him for being out of contact. Holding his phone with one hand, he used his teeth to pull the glove off his other hand then felt around in the snow until he found his keys. Shivering, he managed to get the door open and tumble inside. His phone had gone silent and he was about to disconnect, when his boss snarled, "Are you there?"

Through chattering teeth Gus croaked, "Yeah. I didn't get all that, what were you saying?"

Voice rising in fury, his boss roared, "When can you get here?"

Slamming the door, Gus slumped on the stairs and squinted at his pocket watch, "How's six A.M.?" 'Perfectly reasonable,' he thought. More incomprehensible roaring came out of the phone. Gus sat on the stairs, waiting for the man to stop yelling. Finally, he was able to explain, "Boss, I can hardly stand up. If I come in now I'll probably plow down a light post without even noticing. Eight A. M. is the best I can do."

Another roar followed, ending with, "You said six before."

Gus drew in a deep breath and asked, "How about seven?"

There was an exasperated snarl, then his boss said, "All right but it will be twelve hour shifts until this storm blows itself out." Gus mumbled, "OK," and hung up.

Lurching upstairs, he peeled off his wet clothes and climbed into a hot shower. Half an hour later, he wobbled back downstairs into the kitchen and poked his head into the fridge. He slid a bowl of something into the microwave, then turned on the computer and found a weather page. Retrieving the, now hot, bowl of something and finding a spoon, he sat down to watch the forecast. Climbing back up the stairs, he carefully checked that his alarm was set for half past five and that the ringer was on maximum volume, then fell into bed.

Smacking the alarm's off button, Gus forced himself out of bed and dragged on warm clothes. On the bus he huddled around a cup of coffee, trying not to fall asleep and miss his stop. Because he started later than most of the others, Gus was put onto clearing foot-deep snow from residential streets, a nerve-wracking job which demanded precision driving. By six o'clock that afternoon, the constant cups of coffee were no longer keeping him sharp, so he was very thankful to be let off shift early, with a stern warning to be in by five the next morning.

Ringing was coming from his locker as he approached; Gus managed to grab his phone before the call went to voicemail. Panting a bit he said, "Hi Lee, I haven't been answering because we're not allowed to have our phones in the truck. I'm so glad you called."

Natalie's voice came from the speaker, assuring him, "The first chance I get, I'll tell Lee how genuinely glad you were, when you thought she was calling. In the meantime, you need to get in here."

"Nat," he said desperately, "it's really going to have to wait. I'm totally wasted, I have to go home and sleep."

"No, there are a couple of things you have to sort out. Here. The Environmental Watch office is open 'til nine."

His protestations went unheard. He fell asleep on the bus, missed his stop and had to walk back three blocks to the EW building. Bone weary, he dragged the office door open against the wind and staggered through. Inside, he was met with a huge hug from a buxom, blond woman. Startled, he said "Hello."

The rosy-cheeked woman clung onto his arm, propelling him towards Natalie, announcing, "Here he is." Facing him again, she declared, "I'm Gemma. I met your girlfriend." He looked at Natalie in bewilderment.

Natalie smiled and said, "Remember the email?" In response to his baffled look, she added, "The waterlogged letter? The washed-out email address?"

"Oh, that email," he murmured. "That was weeks ago."

"Yes. I was on a high mountain hiking trip," Gemma chimed in. "No internet up there, so I only saw it last week."

"You need some coffee," put in Natalie, guiding the three of them to the snack table.

"Some friends were coming up here for the pumping station demonstration, so I hitched a ride. I got here Saturday morning. You weren't here," Gemma said, looking at him accusingly. "I crashed with my friends, then we went to the demo. Your girlfriend was introduced at the legal briefing. While we were waiting to board the buses, I asked her if she knew where you were. I explained that you had invited me to stay with you." Gus spluttered coffee. Gemma rushed on, "I didn't know she was your girlfriend. I know I shouldn't have exaggerated but

I didn't want to be alone for Christmas. Later I met Natalie." Her eyes sparkled with joy.

"Gemma's been staying with me," explained Natalie.

"Everything worked out for the best," said Gemma happily, then frowned slightly. "Except your girlfriend might be angry, but that'll be OK. Natalie can explain everything to her."

He coughed to clear the last of the coffee from his throat; looking up at Natalie's anxious face, he said quietly, "That explains things."

"I tried to call Lee just before you came, it went straight to voicemail."

"She'll have flown out by now. Apparently no cell reception at the ranch."

Natalie said, "On a brighter note, come and look at the video clips."

Gemma said to him reassuringly, "I'm sure it'll work out OK." Obviously restraining herself from giving him another hug, she said to Natalie, "I will go and help put the rest of the placards away."

Nodding to Gemma, Natalie sat Gus down at a computer, and began bringing up an internet video feed. He muttered in anguish, "Ah. This is just so not fair. Being with her family is hard to start with; Lee knew they'd be mad about the money, they don't like me and now she thinks I'm bopping some eco groupie."

Natalie snapped at him, "That's an ignorant thing to say. She's a well-respected scientist researching the impacts of climate change on high altitude atmosphere."

Taken aback, Gus said apologetically, "Sorry Natalie, I'm a little raw. What did you want me to see?"

A video appeared on the computer screen, showing the shower of chickpeas he had dropped at the pumping station demonstration. Quickly guarding his expression, he asked, "Is it like that thing in the park? When was that?"

Humphing in disbelief, Natalie said, "As if you didn't know. Look at the number of views."

Scrunching his face a bit he asked, "Is that three hundred 'K'?"

"Yes. Three hundred thousand views of this video alone. There were several different videos of the action posted."

"That's good. I'm glad the demo got a good response," he said, starting to get up.

Natalie put a hand on his shoulder. "That wasn't the best part, watch this." She rapidly typed into the search bar and tapped return. The screen showed a few different clips of the demonstration. He grunted in surprise. Typing again, Natalie brought up several more videos and commentaries.

"Wow. That guy really hit the jackpot," Gus said, working hard to suppress the elation in his voice. "What did you type in the search bar?"

"Looks like two tags are dominating, '#headsup' and '#paintball.'"

"Why paintball? Paintball is like, I don't know, a grown-up version of squirt guns. Not like that shower, is it chickpeas again?"

"Paintball is the viral trend for now." Natalie went on, "If he keeps this up, this guy is going to end up an eco hero."

Somberly, Gus responded, "As long as he, or she, remains anonymous. Lee says if they were caught they could get charged with public mischief and given five years in prison." He gave Natalie an intense look and added, "'You can't tell what you don't know.'"

Chapter Nineteen

Christmas season, for Gus, was a fatigue-blurred week devoid of joy. Once a day he called Lee's phone, hoping there might actually be reception somewhere around the ranch. It was hard for him to understand how her family full of rich, high-powered executives would allow themselves to be out of communications for a whole week. But she never answered.

Every day, tons of wet slushy snow were dumped onto the port; plowing roads was a round-the-clock operation. The course 'students' were supposedly getting 'work experience' while paid minimum wage, and they had to work the same hours as the regular drivers. The storms did not abate as Christmas got closer. Gus ended up working all manner of odd shifts. At three o'clock one morning, he was getting himself coffee and a donut when he ran into Joe. "Hi, how's Dvora?"

Joe replied, "Great. Doctors say any day now we'll be getting a delivery. If the stork can find its way in this weather," he added with a crooked grin. "You look really rough, are you OK?"

Gus smiled at his friend. "Yeah, I'm OK. This weather is supposed to let up soon, and after Christmas the regular drivers will take a lot of the shifts I've been doing."

Joe nodded. "Course supervisor just told me not to come back until Boxing Day and to phone in first, because he might not need me."

Gus agreed, "All the family men are being given time off."

Frowning, Joe said, "Well, no offence, but like I said, you look exhausted. I could take your shift if you like."

Gus asked, "Do you need the money?"

Slightly taken aback, Joe protested, "No. No. It's just that you look as if you need a day off."

With a haggard smile, Gus slapped Joe on the shoulder. "Thanks, but you better stay with your wife. She'll want you in the delivery room, although the way I hear it you'll get cussed up, down and sideways."

Heading towards his truck he called over his shoulder, "Merry Christmas."

Joe shouted after him, "And to you."

Christmas Day, Gus worked a split shift. Midmorning, he tried Lee's number again but it went to voicemail. He left a Christmas greeting, then wondered what to do for the few hours left in his break. Some of the other guys from the course shouted for him to join them. Together, they all went to a nearby diner and had hot roast turkey sandwiches and plum pudding. Even without booze, they had a great time telling trumped-up stories about the course supervisors and describing close shaves. Hunched into their coats, they trudged back to the truck barn with the wind blowing the beginning of another storm in their faces. At the barn, the supervisor told them this was supposed to be the last gasp of the storm cycle, "if meteorologists could be believed." They all found a cot or couch to crash on for a couple of hours before another eight hours in the cab.

Nobody had made it home before Boxing Day, which went much the same way. Gus was glad the port's truck barn had showers, and that he had enough clean, dry clothes in his locker. Finally, two days after Christmas, late in the evening, Gus was told he would have the next two days off unless there was more snow.

Opening his phone, he saw there were still no messages from Lee. He gathered up all his laundry and set off for home. If it had not been for sympathetic bus drivers waking him up, he would have slept through every transfer. Getting off at his last stop, with a word of thanks to the driver, he plodded up his street. No lights were on in the house, but once inside he heard muffled sobs. Dropping his bags and yanking off his boots, he scrambled up the stairs and along the hall to their bedroom. Lee was crumpled up on the bed sobbing in anguish. Quietly, he approached the bed and softly touched her shoulder.

She spun around so quickly that he stepped back. With tears streaming down her face she demanded, "Where have you been?"

"At work."

"Don't lie to me. I called the house yesterday and there was no answer. I got here before noon, and there is food in the fridge that Amy put there days ago. Now tell me the truth. Where have you been?"

"At work. We've been working split shifts and sleeping at the truck barn."

"I suppose that bimbo has been staying with you."

"What...? Oh! You mean Gemma?"

"Yes, the blond hoo-hah with the sexy accent."

"I saw her at the office. The Environmental Watch office, uh, the day you flew out." Realizing his explanation had not helped, he hurried on, "It was all a mistake. I didn't invite her. She even admitted that she made that up. She stayed with Natalie after the demo. I haven't seen her since. Honestly. Perhaps she's still staying with Natalie. Natalie seemed to...you know, like her..." He wound down into silence.

"We'll soon see about that." Glowering at him Lee began to rummage on the bed. Mutely, he pointed to the side table. Scowling at him, she grabbed her phone and punched in a number. Tapping her foot impatiently, she waited for an answer. When it came she said distractedly, "Natalie? I'm sorry I must have dialed a wrong number." Pausing she listened. "She's with her daughter?" Another pause. "Ah yes, yes that's me." Pausing again she said, "I don't want to disturb her." Listening some more, she seemed to be surprised, and then said, "Natalie?" For the next minute she said little but "Yes" or "Oh" as she sank back onto the bed.

Gus went into the bathroom, quietly closed the door, and took a quick shower. Presently he came back into the bedroom and sat beside her on the bed. Tears streaking down her face, Lee wept, "Why didn't you tell me?" He knew it was not the time to complain about cell phone reception. Gus put his arm around her shoulder. With great shuddering sobs, Lee turned into him and cried as if her heart would break. Waiting until she subsided, he gave her tissues and gently smoothed her hair. In a little while, she began to dry her face and, looking at him contritely, said, "I'm sorry."

Not knowing what to say, Gus asked, "How was the week?"

"Ghastly. I have never had such an indescribably horrible week in my life."

Quirking a smile at her he asked, "Want to talk about it?'

She choked on her laughter and pounded his shoulder with both fists, gasping, "It's all your fault, you know. You are a fraudulent money-grubber, leading me into dangerous ways."

"Hmm. Well, this money-grubber is hungry. Want some tea?"

"Yes please. Do we have any bread?"

"Probably stale."

"That's all right. What I really want is toast, with butter and jam."

"All right then, you go wash your face. I'll put the kettle on."

A while later, they sat at the kitchen table drinking warm sweet tea, amongst the debris of breadcrumbs and jam pots. Gus asked, "We knew they would be down on you; did something make their behaviour especially terrible?"

"You were right, they've been spying on me. The stupid donkeys were getting updates on you while I was at the ranch."

"How'd they do that? I thought there was no cell reception or landline."

"They all have satellite phones. There's a two-way radio for emergencies, as well."

"Uh. That makes sense, I only met your father for a couple of hours, but I couldn't see him being out of touch with his financial enterprises for a whole week."

"Oh, good heavens no. Latest in encryption software, best electronic headsets available anywhere. My father conducts as many meetings from the ranch, by sat phone, as he does anywhere else. My mother was gabbing away to her friends who are on a tropical island. I'm the only one who couldn't talk to anybody. I sure as heck wasn't going to give one of them the satisfaction of having me beg to use their phones."

"You said they were getting reports on me?"

"Hah, my loathsome little brother has had us followed since we jammed the bugs. He's very frustrated because the security company can't keep track of you. There are whole days where you disappear. Apparently, they can't electronically track you, because of some sophisticated blocking mechanism on your phone."

"Huh," he snorted. "I take out the battery and SIM card."

"Uh. He's convinced that you're plotting, with a gang of terrorists, to kidnap me for ransom. When he voiced that opinion, my father was kind enough to point out that he will not pay ransom. For anyone."

"Boy, they were full of Christmas cheer."

"It's true though. Last year, an executive slipped his security so that he could visit a mistress and got 'taken.' The kidnappers sent back ears and fingers for several months. My father wouldn't pay. In the end they gave up and dumped the mangled body in front of the corporation's local office. My brother wants me to have bodyguards, which he'd be happy to supply."

"Might keep you safe. Besides, think of the free education those guards would get, sitting in on all your classes."

"No. Uh-uh. No way. I told them too many of my clients would disappear at the least hint of any kind of, uh, 'security.' I'm frightened by how much they know about you though. They told me your whole life story."

"Really? Do they know who my parents are? Because I don't."

"They're still working on it, even though they used a DNA sample. Don't ask me how they got it."

"Holy moly, sounds like we need to keep you safe from them."

"I'm OK, for now, because I'm studying law. For my father, corporate law exists to help corporations. He doesn't even mind that I'll be specializing in compliance with environmental restrictions. He probably thinks that once he brings me around, he'll have an 'in house' expert on how to break the compliance laws."

Yawning, Gus asked, "Mind if I check the weather?"

"Go ahead, I'll clean up," she said, opening the dishwasher as he clicked at the computer.

A few minutes later, he turned the computer off. "Looks like the weather is going to lighten up for a few days, so I won't have to work. Anything you want to do?"

"I threatened to take legal action if my brother didn't stop having us followed. A prof of Rob's is one of the foremost experts on 'privacy of person' in the country, so I'm going to ask him to send a cease-and-desist letter. I'll get the electronic security guys to give me a gizmo so I can sweep locations and make sure I'm not being bugged."

"Oh boy. This sounds like fun. Maybe I should just go back to work," Gus said as they climbed the stairs.

As they got ready for bed, Gus suggested, "I'd like to go out to the Island Hill, and visit with Elder Luke."

"Hmm." Drowsily she murmured, "Let's take Natalie and Gemma out to dinner."

"You want to see if Gemma knows which fork to use?" Gus asked, looking down at her but was already asleep. Putting in his mouth guard he turned off the light and settled into the most relaxed sleep he had had in more than a week.

Chapter Twenty

Soon enough they were back into their routine. Gus's work diminished as the port's weather subsided into its more usual pattern of rain and light snow. Lee disappeared into her books, although Gus still managed to prise her out of the library at least once a week.

One beautiful Sunday found them rolling up to the dock beside Rob's boat, as Natalie began handing out reusable containers of sandwiches and fruit. Barely looking up from her book, Julia took an apple. Gemma looked over Julia's shoulder then said, "That's some pretty sophisticated medical stuff."

"Stuff," said Natalie. "Is that a technical term in Dutch?"

Chortling Gemma replied, "Yes, it means too difficult for you, but Jesse will understand it fine."

Rob explained, "One of those islands I want to sail to has a medical school. Julia hopes she can get into it. Her plan is to do about five years' worth of courses in ten months. If she can, they'll admit her to their two-year program."

Gemma frowned. "An MD program?"

"Yes," explained Julia, "they've compressed the essentials into a twenty-four-month program, which means that I could get an MD degree. It is accredited, although it probably would not be good enough for me to get licensed to practice medicine here. However, it would mean I could be admitted to the university's program on the impact of chemical pollutants on the human body. It's a world class program."

"I told her I could just buy her a degree," drawled Rob. "Anyone can get an MD from an online university, but she seems to think that's cheating. I, of course, have no objection to cheating."

Sensing Julia's exasperation with Rob's attitude, Gus asked, "You're still going to sail off into the sunset then?"

"Well, I'd like to, but the boat needs a lot of work," responded Rob. "I'm going to fix the essentials so we can shake it down with some short sailing trips this summer. Next winter it will have to go into a work shed. Then it can be opened, dried out and major repairs can be done. Trouble is, I can only work on it now and then. Nobody wants to rent me a shed because I would need it for an unpredictable amount of time."

"Isn't there a shed for sale down at the far end?" Lee asked.

"Yes but I can't just buy a shed," said Rob. "I don't have that kind of money."

"I do," was Lee's retort. "Let's go take a look." Catching Natalie's eye, she slightly raised her chin towards Jesse. Getting a smile in response Lee cried, "Come on Jesse, let's race Uncle Rob."

Meanwhile Gemma had been examining Julia's course list. She looked up, declaring, "This really is a huge amount of work. How are you managing with it?"

"Not well," was Julia's despondent reply. "The company I work for is doing an intricate time-sensitive study, Rob wants me to help him with the boat and these courses are not the kind of thing you can just breeze through."

Gemma raised her head to look at Natalie, saying, "I've been thinking I might stay for a

few more months." Seeing a happy smile appear on Natalie's face, Gemma turned back to Julia, offering, "I could help you with these courses. I did a lot of similar courses for my PhD."

"That would be very kind, I could really use the help" admitted Julia.

"It'll be fun. Besides, it'll be a great way to review some aspect of human physiology before I formulate my paper." Gemma pointed to a note Julia had made in a margin and began to explain something.

"You've sure rounded up a lot of volunteers for the Island Church campaign," Gus said to Natalie.

Looking relaxed and happy Natalie responded, "That project generates volunteers for itself. We've had a lot of walk-ins asking to help with it, which is great for EW. We wanted to improve our relations with faith communities."

"Is there anybody who might take up the leadership, do you think?"

"Hmm. There's that youth pastor. She might take it on."

"Can you talk to her about it? I've only got a couple more weeks on my course, then I'll need to be going out to Island Hill and begin preparing the road for the house-moving trucks."

Natalie nodded, about to speak, when Jesse exploded into her arms trilling, "Mommy, Mommy, we saw a big, big, big place. Uncle Rob says he can put his whole boat into it."

Laughing, Natalie hugged her child, exclaiming, "That'll be good because I am freezing out here on this dock."

The group collected up thermoses, wrapped china mugs in napkins and cleaned up their debris before moving toward their bikes. Gemma and Julia were checking schedules on their phones. Natalie settled a suddenly sleepy Jesse into her bike trailer.

Gus and Lee walked on either side of Rob. "You've met Ben, right?" Gus asked. Rob looked puzzled. "Remember Amy, the tall woman?" he asked, holding a hand above his head. "And then there's Ben," he continued, holding his other hand at shoulder height.

As Rob tried to suppress a laugh, Lee leaned forward to tell Gus, "Don't be mean."

Rob nodded in recognition.

"Ben is a woodworking artisan; he could do a lot of the work on your boat."

Before Rob could say anything Lee leapt in, "I'll form a limited company to buy the shed, which can take at least two boats at a time, so I'll hire Ben to supervise. When you have time, you can teach him how to restore boats by giving him work to do on yours. Everybody wins."

"I can't let you do that," Rob complained. "Our fathers will think we're conspiring against them."

Grinning, Lee replied, "Good. Anyway, what's the use of having money if I don't spend it?"

With a 'that settles that' look on her face, Lee swung onto her bike and led their cavalcade out through the marina gates. Everybody called or waved goodbye as they pedalled off towards their homes, except for Rob, whose latest antique car blasted past them in a cloud of exhaust fumes.

Traveling along at a good speed, Lee and Gus were soon able to turn into a residential neighbourhood and ride side by side. The wind put a rosy bloom in Lee's cheeks and streamed her mane of red locks out behind her. Turning her head toward Gus, she caught his look, "What?" she asked in surprise.

"Oh, nothing," he replied, all innocent.

"Hmm. I told you I got a reply from Frederick, right?"

"Who's Frederick?"

"Frits." At his blank look she went on, "Ginger from Plastic Reuse."

"Frederick? I like Ginger better. What'd he have to say?"

"Plastic Reuse is cancelled. Government cut their funding. He and Abigail are thinking about coming west for a few months."

"Abigail? You're kidding right?"

"No, those are their names, Abigail and Frederick."

"Better stick with Blondie and Ginger."

"Uh. Anyway, I thought we might invite them to stay with us for a while, until they sort out somewhere to live."

With a slight frown he said, "It's your house honey, you can invite whoever you want."

"Well, I own it, but you and I living there makes it our home, so I think we should decide things like this together."

Riding along silently, Gus appeared to be mulling over the idea of a home, so Lee waited patiently. Finally, he gave her an anxious look and said, "I've never really lived with anyone before. I don't know how this works."

"Other than my family, who are really the most ridiculous model, I don't have any examples. I haven't really lived with anyone either."

"Hmm. Well, I don't have any models." Gus pedalled along deep in thought until he shrugged, then began to explain, "I'm surprised with how comfortable it is for me to live with you. I like it. I don't want to mess it up. I don't know how I will be with other people in the house, I might withdraw or get surly. Having them come to stay scares me."

"I can see that. Coping with my large, antagonistic family has made me keep my real self inside myself, if that makes any sense." Gus nodded in understanding. Lee continued, "So I shouldn't invite them."

"No. Invite them. Soon, I'll be up at Island Hill a lot, so even if having house guests is a strain, I'll have lots of alone time to sort through my feelings."

A few days later Gus came home to find Ginger and Blondie sitting on the front steps.

"Hey, I'm sorry. I didn't know you guys were arriving today," he said shaking Ginger's hand and giving Blondie a hug.

"Neither did we, things suddenly came together with a ride. Naturally, this big oaf has Lee's email address but no phone number," said Blondie, poking Ginger in the ribs.

"Bring your bags," Gus said, unlocking the door and leading them upstairs. "This is the guest room. Amy should've got it ready with clean sheets and everything. There's a bathroom over here and those towels are for you."

"Man, this is pretty fancy," said Ginger. "Oaf that I am, I hope don't break anything valuable." Snorting Gus said, "What would you like first, shower, cup of tea, a beer?"

"How about shower, then a cup of tea," suggested Blondie.

"OK, I'm going to shower as well."

Ginger said, "OK, you go first. We'll unpack."

"No need, the bedroom has an ensuite bathroom. Don't worry, the water pressure is phenomenal."

Gus pulled out his phone as he went into the bedroom and called Lee but there was no answer. 'Naturally,' he thought and left a message telling her to get her nose out of her books and come home. Showering quickly, he put the kettle on and began laying out some snacks, thankful for the abundance of Amy's provisioning.

Blondie came down first, stepping into the well-used, homey kitchen with apparent relief. "Never mind Frits, so many beautiful things. I'm afraid I'll knock something over."

"You'll get used to it," Gus said, pouring water from the kettle into the teapot. Indicating the food laid out on the table he added, "Sit, help yourself."

In a few minutes, Ginger joined them. The three began catching up and swapping opinions on current events. Presently Gus's phone went off. Looking up from a text he asked, "Do you guys like Thai food?"

"Love it," said Blondie

Gus rapidly typed a return text. "Good, that's supper organized."

Ginger asked, "Do you think we have time for a trip to the laundromat before supper?"

"I think so, it's right down those stairs," Gus said pointing.

"Basement. I forget about basements. Right, mind if we borrow some detergent?"

"Help yourself, it's all unscented environmentally friendly stuff."

Ginger started to get up but Blondie put a hand on his arm. "It'll be easy for me to get a barista job. I'll do the laundry, while you see if there are any websites for finding construction work," she said, nodding toward the computer.

"You do construction work?" Gus asked.

Pulling the computer towards him, Ginger said, "Actually I have a degree in Civil Engineering. Put myself through university driving heavy machines, bulldozers, stuff like that."

Creasing his head in thought, Gus watched Ginger's large fingers fly across the keyboard for a minute, then cleared the table and loaded the dishwasher. Following Blondie downstairs, he made sure she had found everything she needed, then asked, "Is there anything you could do besides working in a coffee shop?"

"Bigger tips in bartending but the patrons of coffee shops are nicer." Glancing at him she added, "You mean what's my real profession?"

"No offence intended. Good baristas are hard to come by."

Smiling, she replied, "None taken. Actually, I have a Bachelor of Science in Agriculture. Next year I want to attend a one-year course at an institute in the Netherlands that specializes in hydroponic farming."

Puzzled, Gus asked, "Vertical farming?"

"Sort of." Blondie finished loading the washing machine, flipped a switch and turned to face him. "Basically, you have long open pipes with water flowing through them. You set your plants at the top of the pipe with their roots dangling in the water, which is actually a sort of lukewarm soup with everything the plants need to grow. Holland is the world leader in this method of farming."

"That's it. I've seen it online. The Dutch, you, use huge greenhouses with rotating racks of plants. Why are you interested in that?"

"If, or I guess, when it is too hot to live at lower altitudes, we think high altitude hydroponic farming, in controlled atmospheres, may be the only way to survive."

There was a commotion of slamming doors and thumping feet from upstairs. Grinning, Gus announced, "Supper has arrived."

As he entered the kitchen Lee asked, "Is it warm enough to eat on the patio?"

Gus nodded, so she put a large tray of tableware into his hands and said, "Wonderful, set the table."

Presently, with a good meal inside them, the four friends were relaxing at the patio table with drinks in hand. Ginger looked inquiringly around and asked, "Do you have a Bar-B-Que?"

Blondie rolled her eyes, explaining, "The inner 'hunter' part of his 'hunter-gatherer' DNA is coming to the fore. Periodically he has to feast on burned flesh."

Laughing, Lee answered, "It's in the garage." Then turning serious she asked, "Do you guys have any work lined up yet?"

"No but we won't impose..."

Lee interrupted, "Not at all what I meant." Looking at Gus she went on, "Ben needs some help at the boat shed for a week or two. It's just paint scraping and stuff but it pays a living wage."

Blondie looked puzzled and asked, "What do you mean, 'living wage'?"

"Political definition," Gus intoned. "One person, working forty hours a week should earn enough to support a family of four, ouch, that hurt," he complained, rubbing his shin where Lee had kicked him.

"Teach you to respect the needs of the working poor," Lee admonished him. Turning to their guests, she said, "It's something over thirty dollars an hour."

"That's very generous," said Blondie.

"That's settled then." Lee frowned, "How will we get you there?"

"I'll take them," Gus said, still rubbing his shin. "The course is pretty much wrapped up, just doing paperwork, it won't matter if I'm late."

"What course?" asked Ginger.

"Heavy machinery operator," Gus said with a quick smile. "I'm hoping you will be able to work with me at Island Hill. We're going to move some houses and, hopefully, a church by putting them on trucks, and taking them from an island in the sound to an inland hill site. Right now, there is a lane from the road, up the hill, to the community. We need to straighten and widen the lane so that it will take two eighteen-wheelers, side by side. Equally important, there needs to be one smooth grade, bottom to top."

Ginger leaned forward, intrigued, "Will the ground bear that kind of weight without extensive foundation rock being laid down?"

"We think so. An engineering firm donated a geological study. The buildings aren't really that heavy by comparison to the kind of loads that can be put on those trucks." He and Ginger got into a technical discussion about how the project would be conducted. Unnoticed by them, the two women cleared the table. A little while later, they returned with tea and began serving pie.

Ginger leaned back. "That's an interesting project. I wish I could see how it would be done."

"That's the thing. I already know we need heavy machinery operators for the lane." He held his hand up towards Ginger. "The whole thing is on private property; you won't need a licence." Looking at Blondie he went on, "You could both live at Island Hill while you worked there. I think they want to build greenhouses. Could you help them with that?"

"Of course, but don't they have greenhouses already?"

"No. To start with, you could probably help with planting a market garden. Later, after we get the buildings moved, we hope to start building greenhouses."

"Sounds wonderful, when can we start?"

"I shouldn't have gotten your hopes up. I'll have to talk to Elder Luke before we can do anything."

"Elder Luke thinks Gus walks on water," Lee put in.

Gus glowered at her and said half seriously, "That was highly inappropriate and you'll notice I didn't resort to violence to convey my criticism."

Laughing, Ginger asked, "Is it a religious community?"

"Yes, is that a problem?"

"Probably not. What denomination?" put in Blondie.

Gus looked at her askance. "Uh, Christian, I don't know. Anyway, I'll come into town and try to separate Lee from her books, most weekends. I can bring you with me."

"Don't worry, we're good at working with people of different religions," said Blondie.

Smiling, Ginger pointed at an open newspaper, "Still doing crosswords I see."

Gus groaned, "And she's a purist, won't let me look up anything online." Laughing, Lee began to read out clues for them all to puzzle over.

Chapter Twenty-One

A couple of Saturdays after Ginger and Blondie's arrival, Ben and Amy pulled up at the house in a rented hybrid van. Gus, Ginger, Lee and Blondie all squeezed into seats then Ben headed towards the highway. Lee asked, "How's the boat shed working out, Ben?"

"A lot better with Blondie and Ginger's help, we're getting everything done."

To Ginger, Lee said, "You've had a couple of weeks to work with this van; what do you think of it?"

"Not enough torque for towing a trailer or even getting uphill with a heavy cargo. Electric motor is finicky too," replied Ginger.

Ben added, "I haven't needed to use the ethanol engine but the battery-operated part is good. I can plug it in to a heavy-duty outlet at the shed and ride my bicycle home. The next morning it's fully charged and ready to go."

"Comfortable," said Blondie. "The seats come out easily and you can really get a lot of cargo in the back."

"Uh. So good enough for a rental but we don't want to buy one for a company vehicle?" Lee asked.

After he negotiated the on-ramp to the highway, Ben, a little deferentially, offered his opinion. "It's not ideal. We would still need to rent a gas guzzler for some jobs."

"This is the only electric van I know of," Lee complained.

"Really?" asked Ginger. "There are several European companies that make this kind of van."

"No dealerships here," Ben pointed out.

"What about, uh, second hand, mmm, used?" asked Ginger.

Ben replied, "I've seen a couple of European models on the road. The trouble is none of us would know a good buy from a total lemon. Plus, there's nowhere to get maintenance done."

Laughing, Gus said "You could open a dealership," but, seeing Lee's thoughtful expression, he quickly added, "I'm kidding. I'm kidding."

Blondie suggested to Lee, "Ginger could help you buy one, he actually knows a lot more about vehicles than he's admitting."

"I could teach Ben enough about the maintenance that you wouldn't need to worry except for something major," admitted Ginger.

"I think I saw an electric van advertised on my message board," put in Amy. "I'll show you tomorrow."

"Tomorrow?" queried Ginger.

"Amy is the deft duster of the many family relics with which my house is cluttered," Lee explained. Then she asked, "How is Rob's boat coming?"

"Great," said Blondie and Ginger together.

Ben explained, "We put it in the water earlier in the week and got it rigged..."

Ginger picked up the story as Ben focused on traffic. "We, 'stood,' uh, 'stepped,' the mast and got it rigged, so we were able to put sail on it. Rob will need new sails before he can go to the South Seas."

"We took it out last night," said Blondie. "It's a very pretty boat and it sails smoothly."

Ginger added, "When it's not going through a plastic patch."

"I was scared," admitted Amy. "I thought if any of the bottles, bags and assorted junk got stuck in the steering, we would end up going around in a circle, all night, before a motorboat could come and tow us out."

"It really upset Rob. He'd never seen a plastic junk float before."

"The plastic problem is worse in the deep ocean, far from shore, where there may not be a motorized boat to pull you clear."

Ben got onto an off ramp, then changed the subject by asking Gus, "So your idea is that the long bed trucks loaded with the houses can be driven up the ramp, get around the curve in this corner, and drive onto the bridge over the highway, and along the tarmac road to the Island Hill turnoff?"

"Seems like a pretty difficult feat to me," commented Ginger, "but then I come from a flat country."

Gus shrugged. "Last year we did a couple of trial runs with empty long bed trucks. We made all the turns, and the ramps are designed for trucks with much heavier loads."

A few minutes later, Ben pulled in at the base of the laneway leading up the hill to the Island Hill community. "Speaking of ramps, torque, heavy loads and such, I think we had better park down here and walk up."

Everybody clambered out and unloaded baskets of food. While they waited for the others, Gus pointed out the features of the island community's new home. Awed, Ginger said, "It could be a Bronze Age hill fort."

"That's partly the clear cutting. With all the forest gone it stands out more. There are several of these flat-topped hills, one behind the other going up into the mountains."

"How high?" Blondie asked as she joined them.

"I don't know exactly. We should check an online satellite map when we get home."

As the group began to walk towards the hilltop, Ginger asked, "How were they formed?"

"Geologists don't really know. This is the only formation with a series of hills leading down from a high altitude."

"Is it some form of esker?"

"Don't know that either. The higher ones all have meandering eskers leading to them. Building roads along those winding paths would be very difficult, so we're lucky to have this straight smooth slope to use, taking the church up to the community."

Lee looked back at Gus and asked, "Will the government close the highway so you can transport the church?"

"Natalie thinks they will. She arranged a meeting for Elder Luke, and a group of faith leaders in a couple of weeks. That youth pastor is doing wonders with the email campaign," he replied.

"Are there a lot of religious people involved in moving the church?" inquired Blondie.

"Oh, thousands by now, I should think," Gus said, nodding. "Being able to draw on all kinds of skills in faith communities is the main reason we can attempt to move the church. Engineers, drivers, old timers who remember how to jack up and move a house. It's quite amazing."

"Divine intervention," murmured Blondie.

"That is certainly what the community members think. They're convinced that living on the high ground will protect them from the coming climate apocalypse. Bearing in mind that they were driven off their island home by floods, caused by climate change, their convictions seem quite reasonable."

As the group arrived at the top of the lane, Elder Luke came forward to be introduced to everybody.

By the end of the day, as Lee, Gus and the others all walked back down to the hybrid van, there was a pleasant conviction that things would work out. The church would be restored to its community and perhaps even the climate apocalypse could be survived, if not averted.

On the drive home Ginger pointed at an overpass and asked Gus, "This is the one the church will have to go under, yes?"

Gus nodded. "It should be OK; we measured carefully."

"And you will drive very slowly," said Ginger with grin.

"Yeah." Gus pursed his lips as they swept under the concrete bridge.

The next months were crammed with successes. Natalie and Elder Luke got government approval for closing the highway. Ginger found two European manufactured hybrid vans, suggesting that Lee buy both of them so that if one broke down the other could be cannibalized for parts. Blondie and Ginger moved up to Island Hill where they were readily included. Ginger did most of the road building, while Gus prepared the houses and church for transport. Amy got accepted to the nutritionist course she wanted, which would begin the following September, and started sitting in when Gemma and Julia were doing coursework. Rob finished his first year of law school. Lee graduated at the top of her class, summa cum laude.

Then things went awry. Friday, a week before the relocation would begin, Gus was looking at the church with Jake, the old-timer who knew how to jack up and transport buildings. Ginger swung off his bike and cheerfully asked, "Why so glum? Glum, it means the same as sad, right?"

"Problem getting the church on to the flatbeds." Said Gus with a grimace, "Major problem."

Ginger's face became serious as Jake explained, "We can put the wooden beams under the houses, no problem. We jack up the beams until the house will be about a foot higher than the bed of the truck, then we back the truck under the beams. We can dig out ramps down to the level of the basement and run the truck bed through what used to be the basement. Still OK. Lower the building, carefully, onto the truck. All good. It'll work fine for the houses. Problem is the church doesn't have a basement."

"Can we get a large crane, or two, and lift the church onto the trucks?" asked Ginger.

"Other places maybe, but not here. We'd have to get the crane onto a barge to ferry it across the sound, which would be extremely risky at best. The weight and height of the cranes would make the barges top-heavy. Any sudden gust of wind could tip them into the water. Doable with the church but not cranes," explained Gus.

"Can we wait, move it later in the year?" asked Ginger.

"Probably not, water level is almost at the top of the berms now. Another three or four weeks, then the warmer temperatures will reach the high mountains causing more snowmelt, which will cause more runoff coming down into the ocean. Plus, we'll probably get storms that will push the ocean water up over the berms, so it's likely the whole island will be underwater. Even now I'm worried about the ground getting too muddy for the trucks."

"Did you just find out about this?"

"Yes," said Gus, looking woeful. "My fault, I looked at the basements in the houses and it didn't occur to me that there wouldn't be one under the church. Stupid of me."

"Stront," grunted Ginger. "Every project hits a challenge sooner or later. How will you make ramps into the basements of the houses?"

"Joe, a friend of mine from the heavy machines course, has one of those small backhoes. We'll use that. I asked him about excavating under the church, but he's pretty sure we would have to make the hole very deep to get the backhoe in. Then the truck would be too low for the church to be lowered onto it. We'll know for sure tomorrow, Joe's bringing the backhoe over to do the ramps. He can only help on weekends; he works construction the rest of the week."

"We'll figure it out. We'll get the beams under the church. Your friend can dig all three ramps for the two houses and the church tomorrow, then on Sunday everyone comes here for a Council of War." Ginger set off toward the houses with the old-timer in tow, calling over his shoulder, "Get Natalie to tell everyone."

Late Sunday morning, Gus and Joe rowed across the sound, from the island back to the mainland. Gus thanked Joe for donating time digging the ramps, and coming Sunday morning to finish the church ramp, then added, "It's good of you to leave your machine with us."

Joe dug his oars into the swell grunting in reply, "Just make sure whoever uses it knows what they're doing."

"Me or Ginger, I promise," Gus said, as they drove the boat up onto the shore where everyone was waiting for them. "Hello to Dvora and the little one," Gus said, jumping onto the beach.

Clambering out after him Joe said, "She'll be glad to see me."
Waving to the group, he set off for the bus stop.

Blondie, making her first trip to the island, said, "A plastic boat."

Jesse looked at her dubiously, "Is not."

Laughing, Blondie scooped her up, and carried her into the boat.
Plunking her down, Blondie told the child, "This seat is called a
thwart.".

"Uh. "Jesse struggled to get her head through the collar of a
lifejacket. "I'm calling it a seat.'"

Gemma sat on the other side of the child. Laughing she said, "Give
it up Blondie, for Jesse things are what she says they are," as she began
to put out an oar. With four oars in the water, and Lee at the helm, the
boat surged across the narrow sound and ran up onto the island shore.
Chattering and laughing, the group walked up the gentle slope to the
church.

"Looks like a rainstorm coming in," said Ben.

"Met forecast says it will blow over by late afternoon," said Julia,
then explained to Jesse that 'Met' stood for 'Meteorological.' Then she
explained what 'Meteorological' meant.

In exasperation Jesse demanded, "Why not call it a weather
report?" She clearly couldn't understand what all the adults were
laughing about.

"Better eat inside the church," said Ginger.

"Is it safe?" asked Natalie.

"Safe as houses." Seeing Amy's expression as she peered at the
excavated ramp, Ginger went on to explain that the beams set under the
church were as solid as the foundations on which they rested.

Jesse ran after Rob who had walked around the corner, then came
dashing back to tell them there was a side door. Everyone helped to
set out the meal, while Jesse scurried about exploring. Fairly soon, she
came back and announced, "This is a pretty boring church, no rooms,
no stairs, and not even a bell tower."

"So," asked Ginger, "War Council first or eat first?"

"Eat is better than talk," Jesse instantly answered.

Bowing to the irrefutable logic of the child, everybody partook of the picnic set out before them. Once they were all settled, Ginger explained the problem with getting the flatbed truck under the church. Summing up he said, "We don't know how to get the trucks under the church. There isn't enough room for the backhoe to excavate."

"The highway closure is set for next Saturday noon to Sunday noon. Not likely we can change the date," said Natalie.

"Wouldn't help if we could, the storm season will start soon and then we won't be able to move anything."

Gus nodded toward Ginger who explained, "The current schedule leaves us very little time. Both trucks and flatbeds are arriving tomorrow, Tuesday we load up the houses and ferry them to the mainland, Wednesday we transport the houses up to Island Hill and set them onto the new foundations. Thursday we bring the empty trucks back. By Friday, we'll have to put the trucks under the church, and load the church onto them. Our goal will be to have the church on the mainland by Friday night, then take it onto the highway and up to Island Hill, by easy stages, starting Saturday. As long as we get the trucks with the church to the Island Hill road by noon next Sunday, we can take as long as we like getting it up the hill and onto the new basement."

"Ironic," drawled Rob.

Jesse, who had been getting increasingly restless, piped up, "What's that mean? 'Ironic.'"

"It is one of Uncle Rob's favorite words, honey," answered Julia with a twinkle in her eyes.

"Yes but what..."

"Look Jesse," said Natalie, pulling a set of bricks out of her bag, "you can build a truck, just like the one that will carry the church."

Diverted, Jesse began to open the set. Natalie turned back to the group and said, unhappily, "We have another problem." Everyone looked at her, "Climate deniers are planning a protest." Amidst a chorus of groans, she went on, "Originally, they were going to block the highway with people. Either they couldn't get a protest permit for blocking the highway, or they couldn't get enough people, so now they're going to dump stuff from an overpass."

"There's only one that we go under," said Gus. "About twenty-five miles out of town."

"What will they drop?" asked Ben. "Rocks or bricks could break the windshield and make it unsafe."

Gemma shook her head, "Police would find anything like that and stop them. Their message boards and podcasts seem to be suggesting dumping stuff onto the church as it goes under the bridge. Eggs, garbage, something like that."

"Or they may copy the Paintballer. It would be easy to fill balloons with paint and drop them onto the church."

Gus asked, "What do climate deniers have against the island church?"

"Unlikely that we'll ever understand," drawled Rob.

"True. How widespread is the call for this deniers' protest?" Gus asked.

The group all looked at Natalie. Finally, she said, "It's only my opinion but I think it will not be a very large turnout. Usually, the deniers get a lot of support from fundamentalist religious groups, but this is a church."

Lee asked, "Could they be relying on word-of-mouth?"

"Seems likely, there's very little online, impossible to know how many people will actually come out," replied Natalie.

"How about if we publicize that we are afraid of a climate denier demonstration?" Gus asked, "Would that motivate a counter demonstration?"

"Not that far out of town. We've got some radio interviews and 'human interest' stories for lunchtime news, where we could casually mention it, but if there is any kind of demonstration the media will love it." Natalie paused. As an afterthought she added, "You know, in the port, there'll be a big turnout to watch the church go up the highway."

Ginger summarized their strategy, "So we ignore it and hope for the best." In response to nods all round he went on, "Now we just have to get the truck under the church."

"Mine will fit," said Jesse, proudly displaying her model. "All I have to do is use my spade to dig a hole for it."

Amid startled looks and chuckles, everyone turned their head towards Ginger. "Is that possible?"

Questioningly Ginger looked at Gus.

"Hand dig a hole big enough for two tractor trailer trucks?" Gus spread his hands. "Worth a try."

"Too late to do anything today."

"First thing tomorrow with buckets and spades."

"Rob and I can bring people from the Island Hill down with the electric vans," suggested Ben.

"We'll need a lot more people than that," said Ginger worriedly.

"Could we put out a call for volunteers?" asked Gemma.

"I volunteer," crowed Jesse. "I've got a bucket and spade."

"You've got school tomorrow," said Natalie severely.

Jesse retorted, "Skip school, save the church."

Chapter Twenty-Two

Next morning, in the pre-dawn light, Gus and Ginger conferred briefly. Ginger began organizing the volunteers from faith communities, who would help to move the two houses. Lee, Blondie and Gemma used the boat to row volunteers and gear to the island. Gus went to the church and began digging. It was soon obvious that the digging was easy enough; getting the dirt hauled away was taking too long. Wheelbarrows were getting stuck in the soft muck of the ramp so earth was being hauled away by the bucketful. Blondie came with the last of the volunteers and watched for a few moments then turned to Ben. "They need yokes, can you make some?"

"Probably, problem will be making them strong enough." He went back with the next boat and left for the boat shed.

Midmorning, a media crew came across with Natalie. They knew a good human interest story when the saw one and promptly began recording Jesse demonstrating how the buildings would be moved, using her model truck and a toy brick house.

In the next boatload Amy brought some huge hampers of food; later Ben arrived with several canoe yokes. Blondie immediately picked up one, settling the central curve around her neck and side pieces onto her shoulders. Nodding, she helped Ben tie a bucket on each end. She went down the ramp in front of the church to get her buckets filled. Then she bent her knees to put the yoke over her shoulders, easily lifting and carrying the dirt away. Blondie handed the yoke and buckets to one of the other dirt haulers, and went to help Ben. The news crew watched then tried to interview Ben and Blondie. Noticing their stricken looks, Natalie came to their rescue. She gave them some quotes, as she shepherded the media crew back to the boat, and saw the reporters and camera crews to their vehicles.

Jesse ran around trilling, "War Council. War Council." The friends all got sandwiches and water from Amy, then gathered on a hummock not far from the church.

A man from the island community group came with Ginger who introduced him, "This is Abe. He is a deacon and can speak for the community."

Looking abashed, Abe allowed, "Not exactly, but I can help with your discussions."

"Good to see you, Abe," said Gus. The others nodded or waved.

"OK," said Ginger, "I can report that the trucks will soon be coming across to the old ferry landing. All the volunteer drivers, flag people and so forth are here. Jonas, their lead guy, is confident they can load up the houses and get them back across the water today. That's all from me."

"I think we should make a rest area for volunteers; set up some tarps, or something for shade. Also, we could also use tables of some sort," suggested Amy, adding, "we might run short of drinking water."

"Flooded out and short of drinking water," drawled Rob. "Ironic."

"That word again," announced Jesse. "What's 'ironic' mean?"

Forestalling a distraction, Natalie instructed Rob, "You shall give Jesse an English lesson this afternoon, which shall feature the meaning of ironic."

In a sensible tone Abe said, "I think the fresh water well is still usable, one of my guys can find out for you. There are piles of planks and poles down by the ferry landing, we can use those to put up sunshade covers."

"I can bring some old sails from the boat shed when I go back to cut some more yokes," said Ben.

Gus looked around at the group. "Good news is the digging is easy enough. The soil under the church is dry and sandy, so it comes out easily. Bad news is we can't carry it away fast enough. We need a lot more people to carry the buckets of earth."

Abe shook his head ruefully. "Planting time at the community. That cannot wait. Anyway, almost all the strong, young people are here already."

"So far we haven't had much response to the call for volunteers. Environmental Watch will leave a skeleton crew in the EV office tomorrow, and bring over everyone else to help here," Natalie added. "That'll only be five or six people though."

"I could ask my friends to come," piped up Jesse.

"Pretty hard work for little people," said her mother gently.

"Yeah, and they'd miss recess," said Jesse, a little forlornly.

"Anything else?" asked Ginger.

There was a general shaking of heads. "War Council is over. Back to work," announced Jesse, running off with her bucket and spade.

"We need a nicer name for these meetings," said Amy.

Several faces were turned to Rob. "OK, OK, I'll work on it," he muttered, raising his hands defensively.

By midafternoon people began to appear on the mainland shore with an assortment of buckets, pails and shovels, all wanting to help dig the hole under the church. The boat crew became very busy shuttling people back and forth from mainland to island. The influx of many hands to help haul away the earth from under the church invigorated everyone. One cheerful, red-faced fellow came puffing up the hill with an armload of canoe yokes.

Spying Ben, he shouted, "I heard you needed some of these."

Ben looked at the yokes and asked, "How did you know?"

"It was on the news," said the man. Shrugging out of a packsack, he pulled out a coil of rope. Together, he and Ben began attaching people's pails to the shoulder-hugging bars. By early evening, all the dirt haulers were given a yoke including the dozen new people who had arrived. Ginger called a halt for the day, and they all trouped down to watch the barges ferry the houses on trucks across the sound to the mainland.

Once the trucks were safely parked on dry land everyone headed home in the gathering dark, tired but hopeful.

The next morning people began arriving at the island with pails and shovels in canoes, kayaks and rowboats. No one had the effrontery to come in a powerboat but there was one sailboat. Blondie began, good naturedly, directing traffic at the island beaches. Gemma turned up with only two people from the EW office, saying that Natalie would come later, adding doubtfully, "Natalie said the phones were going like the 'clappers.'" Looking at the others inquiringly, Rob explained that it meant the phones were ringing all the time. By midmorning, there were nearly fifty people hauling dirt away from the church and even Gus began to feel hopeful.

Natalie arrived with two media crews. Jesse promptly announced she was an 'on the spot' reporter. One of the media producers gave his crew a nod and they filmed Jesse giving instructions on the clothes volunteers should wear. Natalie watched with some apprehension as her daughter informed the camera, "You should wear boots because the seashore is very muddy. Jeans and shirts you don't care too much about, everything gets dirty. Work gloves are good because the buckets are heavy and hurt your hands. A hat and sunscreen are essential." Everybody smiled and clapped as she carried two small pails on her made-to-measure yoke.

Ben and Julia had put up sails for shade, and made tables from planks. Julia and Amy set water containers on the plank tables and then put out a large variety of food. Once Blondie was sure that everybody was getting lunch and lots of water, she asked Jesse to go around and tell everyone there was a meeting.

Abe joined them, suggesting that meetings might be called a 'community council.' Jesse corrected him saying, "Uncle Rob says this is a council of el ronds."

"What are el ronds?" asked Abe.

"Oh, wonderful ancient beings," Jesse explained. "Magic people with long sticks, little people like me, gruff grumbling miners, people with pointed ears that shoot bows and lots of people with swords and axes and things."

"Rob," demanded Julia, "what have you been filling her head with?"

"Only the finest literature in the English language," responded Rob indignantly.

Jesse looked worried, interjecting, "My Mommy says that's the 'spear' man."

"Oh Jesse," laughed Gemma. "What would we do without you?"

Jesse's frown deepened but before she could lead them off on another diversion, Blondie announced, "I had a call from Ginger." Everyone turned to her as she continued, "He says the trucks got the houses to the highway turn-off without any complications. They're expected to start up the island community lane by midafternoon. He is hoping the community members can return early, to help set the houses on their foundations." Winking at Jesse, she added, "Before I agreed, I wanted to ask this council of ronds."

"Sounds good, can somebody take the island people home in the vans?"

"Joshua will go with the rest of the community members back to Island Hill. Tomorrow they'll help with the houses. We agreed that I should stay here to help because of my knowledge of the island," said Abe.

Frowning, Gus said, "I'm worried about the ramp leading to the church."

Blondie nodded. "Under the church is dry but the ramp was muddy to begin with; now, with all of these people carrying buckets in and out, it's turning into a quagmire. Should we lay down boards for them to walk on?"

"That would help," said Abe. "For the people anyway. I'm afraid when the trucks try to pull out with the church, their wheels will just spin in the mud."

"One of those guys who came to help out is a civil engineer, he thinks we need to put down a bed of gravel," commented Ben. "I told him I didn't see how we could bring enough gravel across from the mainland."

"There's a gravel pit on the high side of the island," said Abe. "It has a smooth path leading to it, we can get the people who brought wheelbarrows to bring stone most of the way to the church, then use buckets to spread the gravel onto the ramp. That should pack down and make it firm."

"OK. Ben, introduce Abe to the engineer," directed Blondie.

As the group began to break up, Jesse announced, "Council of ronds, adjourned."

"Poppet, where do you get these words?" her mother asked. Jesse's eyes darted to Rob, then widened in innocence. Natalie laughed.

A short while later, wheelbarrows full of stone began rolling down the path to be dumped onto the surface of the ramp. Volunteers developed a smooth system to dig and carry away dirt, with about a third of them drinking water and resting at any given time. Gus stepped up beside Blondie, as she was coordinating activities. "I've got some things to do. Will you be alright if I leave early?" he asked.

Blondie gave him a penetrating look. "Ja, be careful."

"Always am." He grinned back at her.

Gus trotted down to the beach, and helped push the boat out into the water as it was setting off to pick up another load of volunteers. Lee looked at him inquiringly. The boat soon ran up the mainland beach, and he gave her a quick kiss, saying, "Stuff to do. See you at home." Then he trotted off towards the bus stop.

As he rode the bus, Gus thought hard about the country around the highway overpass that the deniers were expected to use. When he got to his workshop, he checked his multi-cannon, set chickpeas to soak, made seed paper streamers and a sinkable duffle bag. Knowing he had done what he could, he set off on his long circuitous route home.

Wednesday was an inspiring day. An astounding number of volunteers found their way to the island with shovels, buckets and all manner of yokes. Soil practically flew out of the church basement while loads of stone trundled down the path in wheelbarrows, to be added to the ramp and make it into a firm bed for the trucks. Several media outlets sent reporters. Jesse announced another council of ronds. Blondie reported that the first house was on its foundation. She said Ginger expected to complete the second house that afternoon. The drivers and other people on his crew would be able to get a day or two's rest, before they started loading the church on Friday.

Natalie had the only bad news of the day. She informed the group that there would almost certainly be a climate deniers' demonstration of fifty to one hundred people on Saturday. Not wanting to make her sources too obvious, she explained it was likely yellow paint would be used.

Thursday dawned cloudy and when it started to drizzle there were traffic snarls all over the port. Luckily, the rain did not dampen the spirits of volunteer excavators whose colourful rain gear made a dazzling rainbow. By noon, the trucks had returned and were being ferried to the island. The ramp to the edge of the church was a long smooth slope of hard packed gravel. The last of the sandy subsoil was being hauled out of the church and by early afternoon, the rain had given way to a light breeze and sparkling sunshine.

Ginger, Ben, the engineer and the truck drivers were examining the ramp and the space which had been dug under the church. Abe and Jake joined them so that with a lot of nodding of heads, there was a general air of optimism.

Lee, Blondie and Gemma rowed the last of the volunteers to the mainland posing in numerous selfie snaps, which soon swamped social media. Finally, the friends stood in front of the church, awed by what had been accomplished by the goodwill of so many people.

As they stood there, Jesse's high-pitched voice asked if there was going to be a council of ronds because she was hungry and they always ate at councils. They were laughing as they collected up the last of their gear, and headed for the boat. Amy dug out a snack for the littlest rond.

On the mainland, Ben checked one of the electric vans and assured Blondie there was enough charge to get them to the island community and back. Gemma took a sleepy Jesse and got her into Natalie's bike trailer, and the three waved as they pedalled away. Lee and Rob went to get their cars, while the second van was loaded with the sails and assorted gear. Gus slid up beside Ginger to quietly ask, "Be alright without me tomorrow?" Ginger gave him the same penetrating look that he had gotten from Blondie. Gus tilted his head and shrugged deferentially. "Stuff I need to do."

"Ja. Watch out for yourself."

Laughing he told Ginger, "That's what Blondie said."

Just then, Rob roared up in his latest sports car. Sticking his head through the sunroof he asked, "What? It runs on hydrogen and emits water."

Julia, with a smile, said, "I have to give him credit, he's not only gone eco-friendly but he crushed the roadster."

"He what?" asked Ginger, agape.

"I crushed it, old man. You know, a giant crane drops a car in a metal box, a huge hydraulic hammer comes down and squashes it flat." Everyone stared at him open-mouthed. "Well, can't do things by halves, eh? Had to bribe the workers to crush it while I watched. I knew if I just left it there, they'd sell it out the back gate and some other idiot would drive around spewing carbon dioxide for years."

"Couldn't you just refit it with an electric motor?" asked Blondie. "It was such a beautiful car, even if it did burn oil."

"No to the electric motor, I checked but it couldn't be done, too boring to explain why. You can each take this beauty for a spin another time. Righty-oh Julia, in you get."

Lee's silent electric car slid up behind him. Waving goodnight to one another, they all set off for their homes.

Chapter Twenty-Three

Lee scrunched her eyes in the bright morning light as she stumbled into the kitchen. Through the dining room door, she saw Gus bent over the table. "Thought we were going to sleep in and go to the island about seven or so."

"Yeah, couldn't sleep."

"What're you doing?"

"Checking the route for Saturday."

"Why? Uh, never mind." Stretching her neck she asked, "Want some coffee?"

"Got some," he replied, indicating a full cup on the table.

She put her hand around it and announced, "It's stone cold. I'll make some fresh."

Gus grunted in response, and continued to study the roadmaps spread out all over the protective covering on the dining room table. A while later, showered and dressed, Lee came back and placed a pot of coffee and a plate of toasted bagels on the sideboard. "Stop. Eat," she commanded.

Looking up, he laughed. "About done anyway." Taking a bagel, he smeared it with butter and jam, mumbling around his first bite, "I still don't see why I can't have donuts in the house."

"Eeew. Environmentally unfriendly and entirely unhealthy."

He shrugged. "Oh well, I'll get some for lunch. I told you I'm not coming to the island today, stuff to do."

"Ahh, sure. Be careful."

Biting into his second bagel, he asked, "What do you expect to do today?"

"Probably nothing. Natalie's worried there be a lot of spectators which could make things unsafe, so perhaps crowd control."

"Rob said something about a 'live stream.'"

"Yes, becoming very popular at demonstrations. Once video is broadcast, anyone in the world can see what's happening. Aside from publicizing actions, it seems to make people behave more appropriately."

"Yeah, some of the EW people are really into it." Picking up one of the maps he folded it and shoved it into his daysack. Lee filled a travelling mug with coffee and brought it to him. As Gus started to open the back door, she drew him into an embrace and gave him a long kiss.

"Have I forgotten your birthday?" Gus asked.

She laughed. "Sometimes I'm afraid I won't get to kiss you again, for a very long time. Be careful."

"Always am." He waved to George as he pedalled down the laneway. Taking his usual precautions, Gus rode to his workshop. Once there he packed his multi-cannon and other equipment into the sinkable duffle bag, put the bag and his bike into the back of the truck and drove off on the route that would be taken by the church.

One intersection before the overpass the climate deniers were expected to use, Gus parked his truck in a commuter lot. He locked up, got his bike and duffle back from the back and pedalled off over the highway. As soon as he was out of sight of the highway, Gus stopped and studied his map then rode back and forth around the countryside. Satisfied he had a way to his shooting point and safe escape route; he rode down a farmer's laneway and slid his bicycle into some bushes.

Gus pushed on through the scrub until he reached the edge of the wood, overlooking the highway. He backed up a little and sat down. Apprehensively he looked at the overpass he wanted to spray with his multi-cannon. That's a long shot. 'This hill we're on might give us some extra range.' *Wind might blow the streamers onto the bridge, if you're lucky.* Finally, Gus decided to go ahead and cache his duffle bag, as planned, so it would be there when he came back the next day. In the event the deniers showed up, he would fire a streamer to see how far it would go. *If it falls short you can abandon the action.* 'Yeah, then I could just haul the hex-a-cannon and drop it in the river.' He knew that after dumping the duffle bag, he could ride on and rejoin the church entourage at the next highway intersection.

At home in the garage, Gus took down a couple of mountain bike tires from the wall. Not the best for his bike, but he knew he needed better tread to get through the muddy side roads. As he set about putting the tires onto his bike, Lee appeared at the door with a cup of coffee.

Surprised he greeted her, "Thanks, I didn't realize you were home. How'd things go?"

"There was a problem with the trailer. The truck cabs backed the flatbeds down the ramp alright but when the church was lowered onto the flatbeds, the wheels sank into the ground—not enough to touch the foundations but the trucks couldn't pull them out." Gus looked at her worriedly. "It's OK, we figured it out. Luckily, a few volunteers had come to watch. Together we brought up all the lumber from the shore. Ben and Abe dug a slope down to the flatbed trailer wheels then laid the boards across in front of the wheels. The trucks were able to inch the flatbed trailers onto the planks. We had to keep moving the boards ahead of the wheels so the trucks could pull them out. We did it in the end, but it took a long time. The church is on the island by the shore. It will have to be put on barges and ferried across tomorrow."

"We're behind schedule but you got it off the foundation. Well done."

"Ginger called a pre-dawn 'council of ronds' at the ferry landing."

"Um. Do you have an old bicycle helmet I could have?"

Lee rummaged in some boxes, then pulled out a battered gray helmet. "Don't know why I still have it but it'll fit anyone. We used to call it a 'brain box.'"

Chuckling, Gus hung it on a handlebar and stepped into the garden behind her.

"I guess we'd better get to sleep early," said Lee.

"Uh huh," replied Gus, hoping she did not mean it.

Very early the next morning Gus set off for the island on his bike. Lee followed soon after in her electric car. As Gus arrived Julia was taking a sleeping Jesse from Natalie and tucking her into the back of Rob's eco roadster. Meanwhile, Rob, oblivious to Amy's disapproval, was offering around a box of donuts.

"Right, this council of ronds is in session," proclaimed Ginger to a chorus of groans and chuckles. "Seriously, we need to mark out the path to the port road. Once the trucks reach the road, the police will take over directing traffic and provide crowd control. The truck and barge crews have their own organization. Our job is supporting the police by keeping spectators out of their way. Comments?"

Ben raised his head. "There are two trailers under the church. Going around corners could be very difficult. We need to make sure that spectators are well back from the road, especially at corners, so the trucks will have room to pull the church around." Everyone nodded in agreement. Gus snagged another donut from Rob and looked at Ginger who shrugged and said, "Nobody's done this before, we'll just have to see how it goes."

Around a mouthful of donut, Gus asked, "What about tomorrow, getting off the highway and up the Island Hill lane?"

"Let's deal with that when we get there."

Gus nodded. The group broke up and went to get the route marked out with pylons. Ben found Abe and brought him up to speed. Rob set off with one of the hybrid vans to pick up Elder Luke and some members of the island community. Natalie helped the media people set up a good shot where they would not obstruct the passage of the church. Julia studied for one of her medical courses, and kept an eye on Jesse who slept through it all.

As it happened, the trucks towed the church off the barges without incident, negotiated the corners without apparent difficulty and by midmorning were making slow but steady progress up the highway. The beautiful day encouraged crowds of well-wishers to throng the route, cheering and creating an atmosphere of celebration. Elder Luke was broadcast leading a prayer of hope. Making up for lost time, by early afternoon the trucks had left the port and were passing through farming country. The crowds had been left behind and most of the volunteers had gone home.

Police blocked off a lay-by, allowing the drivers to pull the church off the road and get out of the trucks for a while. Amy had laid out a large buffet with the help of Rob and Jesse. All the flagmen, even the police officers, were relaxing and enjoying the meal. Traffic was flowing past, waving and honking in support, giving everyone a feeling of hope. Natalie was allowed through the barrier by a police officer and quietly called a meeting, while gathering a meal for herself.

The group unobtrusively drifted together, except for Jesse who was tearing about as usual. A perceptive police officer asked Natalie's permission, then invited Jesse to see the inside of his cruiser. Julia had been driving Elder Luke home, and pulled in just as Natalie began to speak.

"Sorry guys, we have a problem." Everyone hushed and waited for her to explain. "The deniers are gathering at a coffee shop just down the secondary road that we have to drive under with the church."

"I think all of the reporters have left, at least none of them came to get a meal," said Amy. "Unless it's on TV it really won't matter much."

"Unfortunately, I was tipped off by one of the TV reporters. They're up the highway looking for a good location to shoot from, as we speak."

Blondie shrugged, "Nothing we can do about it, so ignore it, and let the police do their job."

"I'll warn the drivers," said Ben. "I don't want them blinded by paint on the windshield."

Rob put in, "The live stream isn't working so well along here, but I can definitely record anything that happens so we can put our own version on the internet."

Jesse flew into Natalie's arms, "You should see the cruiser Mom, it's got a computer and everything." Looking around she said, "No fair, you can't have a council of ronds without me."

Gemma slid in to take the child from her mother announcing, "Dessert, that's what we can't have without you."

With somber expressions, the group broke up. Ben went to talk to the drivers while Natalie searched out the senior police officer. Gus walked toward the back of the flatbed putting an arm over Rob's shoulder. "I rode up and down this highway for months when I was going to the heavy machinery school. Just beyond the overpass, on this side of the highway, there's a hill that would be the best place to get a shot of the protest. It's got a cell tower on it so your live feed should work."

"Oh Kaay," answered Rob in a puzzled tone.

"Maybe you could go on ahead and show it to the media people. That way they will keep their cameras pointed down the highway."

Light dawned in Rob's eyes, "Right oh. Best of British luck, old boy!"

Gus continued on to the back of one of the flatbed trailers and unstrapped his bike. He was lifting it down when Lee pulled up beside him in her hybrid car. "Strap your bike on the back. I've got lots of battery charge left."

Easing the car out into traffic, Lee was silent while she drove up to the next interchange. Gus pointed out a where to stop. He was about to get out when Lee leaned over and gave him another long kiss.

As he swung onto his bike, Lee tossed him his helmet. "Don't forget your 'brain box,' be careful."

"Always am!" He gave her a wave as he sped off up the road. Following the route he had scouted the day before; he went along the famer's laneway then got off and locked his bike to a tree. He trotted into the woods and crawled to the tree line so that he could see the whole area. Across from him, closer to the overpass, were several media crews; it looked as if Rob were holding forth about something. He could just imagine Julia rolling her eyes.

On the bridge, he could see that an orderly crowd was gathering. Police had cruisers at both ends of the overpass but, having no reason to intervene, they were monitoring the situation and directing traffic. Looking past the bridge, Gus could see the trucks slowly but steadily pulling the church up the highway. He estimated that it would be about five minutes before the crowd would start throwing things. 'How much wind is down there?' wondered Gus. Just then a police officer sneezed and his paper tissue was caught by the wind and blown towards the center railing of the bridge at a brisk steady speed. *Excellent wind gauge. Almost as if he did that on purpose.* Lining up the multi-cannon, Gus fired the first streamer, which came down almost perfectly in the middle of the overpass.

Elated, he rapidly rained chickpeas down on the crowd who scattered dropping paint bombs and signs all over the bridge. The fifth air cannon exploded, fortunately blowing the sharp metal air pressure valve away from him. Alarmed, he still managed to get off the last canister of streamers. Backing out of the brush, Gus turned and ran straight into a woman who was standing behind him.

"Good shooting," she said. Grabbing his daysack and duffle bag she ordered, "Follow me," and set off along the track at a rapid pace.

Too shocked to do anything else, Gus ran along behind her. To unlock his bike, Gus had to drop the multi-cannon. The woman grabbed it and began shoving it into duffle bag. Gus looked frightened. She grunted and said, "If I wanted to turn you in, I would've already called 911."

She threw the bag into the back of a battered old pickup truck and told Gus, "Get in." Gunning the truck up the lane, she turned away from the highway informing him, "I can drop you at the road parallel to the highway that goes up across the river."

Gus gave her an appraising look. He saw a fit, sunburned, young woman in frayed jeans and a plaid shirt. Cramming the 'brain box' on top of the hex-a-cannon, he fastened the top of the duffle bag then asked, "Why would I want go there?"

She gave him a 'how dumb do you think I am?' look then answered, "That duffle bag weighs a ton and has holes at the bottom. Only reason for that would be so it will sink fast when you drop it in water."

Gus looked at her thoughtfully for a minute. Finally, he said, "Yes. The corner of the parallel road would be great."

"That was pretty cool back there."

"Thanks. Mind if I ask you something?"

"You can ask."

Grunting in amusement, Gus went on, "Why are you helping me?" She stared through the windshield for so long, he thought she was going to ignore the question. Finally, she slowed her beat-up old truck and glanced at him, then spoke in a harsh voice, "I'm the seventh generation of my family to be born on this land. My grandfather was stubborn as a mule and managed to stay competitive while the food-producing corporations bought up most of the land around here. You're lucky my father didn't see you poking around in our woods or he'd have blasted you with his shotgun and asked questions afterward. He's smart, in a way, so he kept the farm profitable by using fertilizer and pesticides and other modern methods. I can't get him to understand that the chemicals are destroying the atmosphere and without bees, we're all going to die. Dad just asks, 'is that what they taught you at that fancy Aa-gree-cul-ture school I paid for?'"

She drove on in silence for a few minutes, then went on, "I know a lot of those people who were down there on the bridge. They're good people. They mean well. It's that they think blaming climate change on the way they farm is just a new way to drive them off their land." She sighed heavily, and then with a grim expression, concluded, "I want to farm this land. I want to have kids and raise them on it. Things have got to change or our grandkids will be burnt to a crisp with everything else."

She pulled over at the crossroad. Gus got down and slung the duffle bag over his shoulder then lifted out his bike. They looked at one another through the cab window for moment then she drove off and he pedalled away.

Chapter Twenty-Four

The rest of Gus's plan went smoothly. He managed to drop the duffle bag into the river when nobody seemed to be around. Although, Gus thought wryly, he had not seen the woman while searching for a firing point. He was pleased to see the bag sink swiftly into a deep, slow-moving, muddy part of the river.

There was a short line of cars at the intersection when he rode up, so he pulled over on the overpass and watched the church move ponderously up the ramp and then down the other side and back onto the highway.

Catching up with the church as it was pulled into another lay-by, Gus was glad to see everyone assembling around another of Amy's meal tables. Jesse ran towards him shouting, "Did you see it? Did you see it?"

"See what?" he asked with an air of innocence that he thought might fool Jesse, but probably nobody else.

"Paintballed. The people got paintballed and ran away!" Frowning Jesse added, "There were kids there and they looked pretty scared."

"Hmm, that's too bad. Was anybody hurt?"

"I don't know. Bet the police man knows, I'll go ask him."

As Jesse scampered off Gus said to Natalie, "Remind me to talk to you about outreach to farming communities." As Ginger approached, Gus asked, "How is our security for tonight?"

"We're good," replied Ginger. "The drivers always sleep in their cabs anyway. Rob is staying to work on his live cam thing, and a bunch of students are having a campfire with a singsong. The police are leaving a cruiser, and the highway patrol officers will stop in for coffee whenever they go by, so the whole place will be active all night. I just hope the drivers can get enough sleep."

Lee came up and gave Gus a quick kiss, then tucked her arm into his. To Ginger she said, "Can we go home and get a good night's sleep?

You know, so we'll be bright-eyed and bushy-tailed for your pre-dawn council."

By then, the whole crew was standing in a loose circle. Ginger looked at Ben and asked, "If we leave at sunup will we get to the turnoff in good time?"

"Yes, I drove up and looked at those corners again. We should be OK coming off the highway, but I'm worried about the lane up the hill."

"Let's get there first, then we can solve that problem," said Ginger.

"Anybody need a ride back to the port?" asked Gemma.

There was a general shaking of heads. "What about you Julia?" asked Ben.

"I have permission to drive the high-performance vehicle, provided I turn on the four-way flashers and don't go over twenty miles an hour," replied Julia with a smile.

The group broke up with smiles and chuckles as they headed towards their cars.

The next morning, Gus drove while Lee dozed in the passenger seat. He used the car radio to scan through the local news broadcasts. The coverage about the church was good, but there was almost no mention of the deniers' demonstration being broken up by a rain of chickpeas.

At the lay-by, supporters were milling around excitedly. Lee awoke and asked muzzily, "What's up?"

"Don't know," he replied, looking for damage to the church or trucks. Natalie was waving to get their attention, so they climbed out and went over to join her. Gus, seeing that Amy, with her usual efficiency, had set up a breakfast table, detoured to collect a coffee but was disappointed by the lack of donuts. He settled for muffins. By the time he caught up with Lee, she was as excited as Natalie. He offered her a sip of his coffee saying with insincere regret, "I'd have brought you a yogurt, but I couldn't juggle it with the muffins."

She waved off his silliness and pointed at Natalie's tablet. He glanced at the screen, then stopped joking around and focused intently for a couple of minutes. Looking up, Gus raised an inquiring eyebrow at Natalie.

"At least three video clips of the 'paintballing' were posted, plus Rob's, which is the longest and most complete. Response is about ninety-nine percent positive. Comments, which is the real indicator of engagement, are rolling in at a rate of five per minute. Editors kept the TV coverage, of the denier demonstration off the air last night but my contacts tell me it will be featured on at least one local Sunday morning talk show. We may even get a little bit of national attention."

Gus dipped his head in acknowledgement and walked off toward the trucks calling, "What needs to be done Ginger?"

Natalie turned a distressed face toward Lee who reassured her by saying, "It's all right Nat. He's used to being alone. The support of a group kind of overwhelms him sometimes."

There was a flurry of activity as police cruisers closed off the highway, flaggers left to help with traffic control at the next intersection, the trucks got rolling and the whole cavalcade moved off up the highway. As Ginger had predicted, the church was being towed up the last ramp well before noon. Everybody watched anxiously as the drivers edged their cabs around the corner at the top of the ramp, guiding the flatbeds carrying the church onto the tarmac road that led to the Island Hill turnoff. There was a collective sigh of relief as the trucks got around the corners and pulled into a rest area.

The atmosphere was relaxed, almost a party, as people got sandwiches, snacks and drinks. Most of the volunteers would be leaving after lunch, some with long distances to drive before reaching home. Gus got his inevitable coffee and begged a couple of illicit donuts off a volunteer before joining Ginger, Ben, Jake and Abe, who were talking with the drivers. Everyone was confident that less than an hour's driving would get the church to the base of the Island Hill's lane.

However, there was a growing concern about towing the church up the steep track. Gus saw a familiar figure approaching and broke away from the group to shake hands with Joe.

Joe indicated the group and asked, "I had a look at the, uh, gravel road, up the hill? Your group worried about that?"

Gus asked, "Yeah, got an idea?"

Joe nodded. "Can I tell the whole group?"

Gus hesitated for a second, and then said, "Sure." He led his friend over and introduced him to the group. "Most of you know Joe. On the island, he excavated the ramps for us. He has a suggestion about how to get the church up the hill."

There were a couple of waves of greeting, then Joe started by saying, "I don't think the trucks can pull the church up the hill." There were several gloomy nods of agreement. "I suggest the trucks tow the two flatbeds up to the beginning of the hill, then we rig a towing bar between the two flatbeds and put a tracked bulldozer at the front to pull the church up the road." There were some frowns and shaking of heads. "And," continued Joe, "put two more tracked dozers at the back, one behind each flatbed, with their blades raised so they can push the trailers if needed or stop them from sliding back."

There was a lot of jaw-rubbing and hand-wringing but in the end, it was the truck drivers supporting Joe's suggestion that settled the issue. Once the church had been pulled to the bottom of the hill, Joe's plan was put into effect.

Natalie shepherded the few remaining journalists to a vantage point, well off to one side of the lane, where the Island Hill people and the last of the volunteers had congregated. Jesse offered an 'on the spot' report by saying that the church was 'being lifted up to heaven by three tanks.' This combination of military and religious symbolism got an amused response, which relieved a good deal of tension.

Joe, Gus and Ginger got their machines into the lowest possible gear and began inching up the hill. Ben's smooth, calming manner helped the three drivers keep the tracks of their machines advancing slowly up the hill. After two grueling hours, the church rolled over the lip of the hill.

The flatbeds were kept moving steadily along the flat hilltop toward the foundation which had been prepared for the church. By the time the drivers began to inch into the foundations the entire community and all the remaining volunteers were watching, with bated breath. As soon as the cross beams holding up the church were in position the bulldozers stopped moving. Jake and three other old-timers went under the church to set house jacks at the four corners. When Jake signalled, the two flatbeds were dragged out from under the church.

There was a collective sigh of relief and a prayer of thanks lead by Elder Luke . Everybody joined together in a huge feast of thanksgiving. Gemma and Natalie sat with Jesse between them. Jesse was working her way through a second helping of pie and ice cream, when she pronounced that 'heaven must be just like this.'

As fiddles and banjos were brought out and space was made for dancing, Lee slipped away from the table to join Gus and they stood gazing at the church, outlined by the golden rays of sunset.

Chapter Twenty-Five

A week later, Jesse bounced along the dock beside Rob's boat and announced to the group, "I have a secret but I can't tell 'til everyone's here." Gemma came along behind her, swung her up like an airplane and 'flew' her to the end of the dock where they looked for fish in the water. Natalie followed with a hamper of food and her ever-present tablet. Spreading out around the open area onboard the yacht, everyone found a comfortable place to sit and chat while they ate.

Lee had been accepted into law school, which gave Rob an excuse to chortle, "Oh boy, a froshie to torment." Julia glared at him, then announced she had early acceptance into her med school, contingent on completing the course requirements. Amy said she wanted to continue doing the courses with Julia. Gemma promised to tutor them over the internet while she was finished her research paper. Blondie promised to email about what she learned from her study of hydroponics. Natalie smiled happily, and told them she would be on leave from Environmental Watch and taking a course in media management.

The five women looked expectantly at the men.

"Whaaat?" queried Rob, "You already know I'm going into second year of law."

"They're just afraid you'll sail away without them," said Ben. "They don't know how much work I need to do, to restore the original beauty of this boat."

"Ah, I am going to the mechanical engineering course, to study flood management," offered Ginger.

Jesse, who, as usual, had consumed an immense amount of food much faster than anyone else, had been playing with the steering wheel. Tugging it back and forth, she called out, "Hey, Uncle Rob, why doesn't your wheel have handles?"

"They're called spokes, honey," said Julia. She nudged Amy and whispered, "And we're sitting in the cockpit,"

"Oh, oh, I remember," cried Jesse bouncing up and down. "Mom, all the ronds are here. Can I tell the secret now?"

"Yes," replied Natalie and Gemma simultaneously. Startled, they looked at each other then grinned.

"I'm going with my moms, Natalie and Gemma, to live in the Ne. The Ne. Urgh, in the 'lands.'"

Failing to understand why a happy burble of congratulations were offered to Natalie and Gemma, Jesse demanded, "OK, spokes. Why doesn't this steering wheel have spokes?"

"Only pirate ships have wheels with spokes," drawled Rob with a nasal twang.

Gus kept the distraction going by asking, "How are you getting to the, mmm, 'lands'?"

Jesse's eyes widened and she looked towards Gemma, who responded, "We don't know yet. Definitely not flying, and even cargo ships contribute a lot of pollution to the atmosphere."

Blondie put in, "Ginger and I will be returning sometime soon as well. We're thinking about sailing but it takes a long time going around either South America or Africa."

"The way things are going you'll be able to sail through the Northwest Passage soon," said Ben with a dour expression.

"Yeah, they've already got cruise liners going along the Arctic coast," put in Julia.

"Sailing close to Antarctica has been dangerous since the times of Drake and all those other quote-unquote explorers from Europe. Can't imagine that climate change is going to make the weather any better for sailing," observed Rob.

"We could ride across North America, then sail to Europe," said Ginger thoughtfully.

"What? On bicycles?" asked Amy. "That would take forever."

"Actually not," said Blondie. "There are tourist trips that cycle across the continent in about two months."

Natalie wrinkled her forehead, then reached for her tablet. "I saw something about an eco-group transporting merchandise by bicycle. Just to prove it can be done. Leaves in about a month." She looked at Gemma who nodded.

"I know of some east coast shipyards that pay people to sail yachts to European buyers. It's faster and cheaper than transporting them by ship. I could make some calls," offered Lee.

"Yeah, all good but let's not waste this beautiful afternoon breeze," said Rob and everybody helped to raise and set sail until they got away from the dock. As the wind filled his canvas, Rob turned up the coast. "Doesn't get much better than this," he said contentedly.

"Won't ever get better than this," said Gus, "Most of us have known one another for a year or more. Nothing has gotten better."

"Some eco-friendly politicians have gotten elected," suggested Amy.

Julia looked at her, responding, "True, but how long before they are a majority, and can change the laws?"

"I agree with Lee on that. The best laws in the world are no help if they're not enforced," put in Ben, as he fiddled with a satellite dish.

"Wait 'til you see the plastic float just up the coast from here."

"We're going to try and livestream a video of it," said Rob.

"Can I be your 'on the spot' reporter Uncle Rob?" asked Jesse.

He looked toward Natalie, but she was absorbed in something on her tablet. Gemma smiled and nodded. After a moment's hesitation Rob replied, "Sure you can. You're a great reporter."

As they sailed toward a miles-wide glob of floating plastic, Lee took over steering from Rob who went to help Ben with the camera and satellite dish. "How can there be so much plastic out here? Much worse than Europe. Does it all wash down from the rivers?" Blondie wondered aloud.

Julia shook her head, "Rob's been researching; a lot of it is just dumped by corporations. Cheaper than recycling it. Also fishing trawlers just cut loose tangled fishing nets and let them float away."

"We need to tack or we'll end up sailing into that mess," said Lee, calling louder, "Get ready to tack everyone."

"What's 'tack' mean?" asked Jesse.

"Means we turn that way, starboard."

"You mean right."

"OK, we undo the ropes holding the sails then turn right and the wind catches the sails and pushes us along."

"Yeah. How does it do that anyway? The wind's blowing in our face and we still go towards it."

"Your Uncle Ginger is an engineer. I think he's the best one to explain that to you."

"Oh thanks," said Ginger laughing. "Explain lift and Bernoulli's principle to a youngster."

Rescuing him, Julia said, "Here Jesse, you can help me with the ropes on the boom."

"That big stick would sure make a 'boom' if it hit my head," exclaimed Jesse.

The friends passed a long, pleasant afternoon, tying up at the dock in the early evening. Gemma picked up a very tired Jesse and carried her ashore, murmuring, "Time for the littlest rond to get some sleep."

"Before you go guys, I wanted to show you this," said Natalie. She displayed a picture on her tablet and everyone clustered around her to get a look.

"Isn't that the pumping station? From the pipeline demonstration last Christmas?" asked Amy.

"Yes, but what am I supposed to see?" asked Rob.

"The flowers," said Ginger.

"The oil company planted flowers?" asked Julia.

"Doubt it. Could it be the chickpeas?" wondered Blondie.

"Don't think so, those look like morning glory and those sprouts might be sunflowers," put in Ben.

"Cool way to remind everyone about us being there, if that's what it is," said Gemma.

Gus leaned in to look closely at the screen then asked, "Looks as if this photo was taken from up a hill. Who posted it?"

"The First Nations who were part of the demonstration. It's being reposted so often that even if the corporation gets rid of the flowers with defoliant, they won't be able to suppress the negative attention they're getting. " Natalie smiled in triumph.

With a sleepy smile, Jesse murmured, "Those are pretty. I hope more get planted."

Author's Note

The idea for this novel occurred to me several years ago in the pre-Thunberg era. Since nobody was paying any attention to the environment anyway, I put off writing this book until I retired. Over the course of the year, in which I wrote *Paintball*, the first version of this book, Greta did a magnificent job of mobilizing people around the world to demand action that will preserve a climate in which humans can live. In my head, this story would not reset into the context of Fridays For Future so I left it set in what I think of as blissful ignorance. I wasn't ignorant; I should have done more. Much more. *Killing Our Grandchildren* is a rewrite of *Paintball* without the boring bits. My hope is it finds an audience and helps to rally old people who can use their votes and their money to reduce carbon emissions.

Don't Try This At Home

I have no idea if any of the stuff that Gus uses in this novel would actually work. I fired a paintball rifle once and concluded it had neither the range nor the accuracy for my story. I suppose almost everyone has played with squirt guns but I don't know if they could be used to shoot green goop. Everything I know about air cannons was gleaned from videos on the internet, so I have no idea what materials you would need for a real version of Gus's cannons nor how to fire them safely. This book is wholly and completely a work of fiction.

These characters are reacting to global warming information that is about a decade out of date. Things are much worse now.

Acknowledgments

Norman Hall, author of Four Stones, my oldest friend, for his unflagging support and encouragement as I blundered through drafts. I also want to thank the folk at Plume Press; Tali Voron who keeps everything on track, and Reilly Ballantyne who converts my clunky pictures into fantastic covers.

Kathleen Brenan, without whom you would be distracted by an endless stream of incorrectly placed commas, quotation marks, grammatical errors and even misspelled words that spellcheckers don't catch. In addition, her thoughtful insights and detailed explanations are a great help in making the characters more real.

Thanks to the Librarians at the local public library who scour the interlibrary loan service to feed my addiction to reading. Also, to Algonquin Coffee which provides the essential fuel for my endeavours. And finally, to the many people in my small town who 'look out' for me, and especially the Red Brick Café crew for refusing to allow me to hide in my house.

Connect with Peter Brickwood

Facebook: https://www.facebook.com/peterbrickwoo

Twitter: http://twitter.com/peterbrickwood

Email: peterbrickwood@gmail.com

About the Author

Peter Brickwood is a crotchety old introvert who started writing novels for the fun of it. Two cats, which he has somehow acquired, graciously permit him to live in a hundred-year-old house that has no lack of things to fix. Building Lego, with kids at the local library, is a great pastime. Otherwise, he is a voracious consumer of books, movies and arcane bits of information mined out of the internet.

CPSIA information can be obtained
at www.ICGtesting.com
Printed in the USA
BVHW040031151122
651950BV00001B/36

9 798215 430286